SHADOW

SHADOW

Michael Morpurgo

FEIWEL AND FRIENDS

NEW YORK

A Feiwel and Friends Book
An Imprint of Macmillan

SHADOW. Copyright © 2010 by Michael Morpurgo. All rights
reserved. Printed in the United States of America by R. R.
Donnelley & Sons Company, Harrisonburg, Virginia. For
information, address Feiwel and Friends, 175 Fifth Avenue,
New York, N.Y. 10010.

Library of Congress Cataloging-in-Publication Data Available

ISBN: 978-0-312-60659-6

Originally published in Great Britain
by HarperCollins Children's Books

First published in the United States by
Feiwel and Friends, an imprint of Macmillan

Book design by Ashley Halsey

Feiwel and Friends logo designed by Filomena Tuosto

First U.S. Edition: 2012

10 9 8 7 6 5 4 3 2 1

mackids.com

For Juliet, Hugh, Gabriel, Ros and Tommo

PREFACE

This story has touched the lives of many people and changed their lives too, forever. It is told by three of these people: Matt, his grandfather and Aman. They were there. They lived it. So it's best they tell it themselves, in their own words.

WHEN THE STARS BEGIN TO FALL

Matt

None of it would ever have happened if it hadn't been for Grandma's tree. And that's a fact. Ever since Grandma died—that was about three years ago now—Grandpa had always come to spend the summer holidays at home with us up in Manchester. But this summer he said he couldn't come, because he was worried about Grandma's tree.

We'd all planted that tree together, the whole family, in his garden in Cambridge. A cherry tree it was, because Grandma especially loved the white blossoms in the spring. Each of us had passed around the jug and poured a little water on it, to give it a good start.

"It's one of the family now," Grandpa had said,

"and that's how I'm going to look after it always, like family."

That was why, a few weeks ago, when Mum rang up and asked him if he was coming to stay this summer, he said he couldn't because of the drought. There had been no rain for a month, and he was worried Grandma's tree would die. He couldn't let that happen. He had to stay at home, he said, to water the tree. Mum did her best to persuade him. "Someone else could do that, surely," she told him. It was no good. Then she let me have a try, to see if I could do any better.

That was when Grandpa said, "I can't come to you, Matt, but you could come to me. Bring your Monopoly. Bring your bike. What about it?"

So that's how I found myself on my first night at Grandpa's house, sitting out in the garden with him beside Grandma's tree, and looking up at the stars. We'd watered the tree, had supper, fed Dog, who was sitting at my feet, his head heavy on my toes, which I always love.

Dog is Grandpa's little brown-and-white spaniel, with a permanently panting tongue. He dribbles a lot, but he's lovely. It was me that named him Dog, apparently, because when I was very little, Grandpa and Grandma had a cat called Mog. The story goes that I chose the name because I liked the sound of Dog and Mog together. So he never got a proper name, poor Dog.

Anyway, Grandpa and me, we'd had our first game of Monopoly, which I'd won, and we'd talked and talked. But now, for a while, we were silent together, simply stargazing.

Grandpa started to hum, then to sing. "*When the stars begin to fall . . .* Can't remember the rest," he said. "It's from a song Grandma used to love. I know she's up there, Matt, right now, looking down on us. On nights like these the stars seem so close you could almost reach out and touch them."

I could hear the tears in his voice. I didn't know what to say, so I said nothing for a while. Then I remembered something. It was almost like an echo in my mind.

"Aman said that to me once," I told him, "about the stars being so close, I mean. We were on a school trip down on a farm in Devon, and we snuck out at nighttime, just the two of us, went for a midnight walk, and there were all these stars up there, zillions of them. We lay down in a field and just watched them. We saw Orion, the plow and the Milky Way that goes on forever. He said he had never felt so free as he did at that moment. He told me then, that when he was little, when he first came to live in Manchester, he didn't think we had stars in England at all. And it's true, Grandpa, you can't see them nearly so well at home in Manchester—on account of the streetlights, I suppose. Back in Afghanistan they filled the whole sky, he said, and they felt so close, like a ceiling painted with stars."

"Who's Aman?" Grandpa asked me. I'd told him before about Aman—he'd even met him once or twice—but he was inclined to forget things these days.

"You know, Grandpa, my best friend," I said. "We're both fourteen. We were even born on the same day, April twenty-second, me in Manchester, him in Afghanistan. But they're sending him back, back to Afghanistan. He's been to the house when you were there, I know he has."

"I remember him now," he said. "Short fellow, big smile. What do you mean, sending him back? Who is?"

So I told him again—I was sure I'd told him it all before—about how Aman had come into the country as an asylum seeker six years before, and how he couldn't speak a word of English when he first came to school.

"He learned really fast too, Grandpa," I said. "Aman and me, we were always in the same class in junior school and now at Belmont Academy. And you're right, Grandpa, he is small. But he can run like the wind, and he plays football like a wizard. He never talks much about Afghanistan, always says it was another life, and not a life he wants to remember. So I don't ask. But when Grandma died, I found that Aman was the only one I could talk to. Maybe because I knew he was the only one who would understand."

"Good to have a friend like that," said Grandpa.

"Anyway," I went on, "he's been in this prison place, him and his mum, for over three weeks now. I was there when they came and took him away, like he was a criminal or something. They're keeping them locked up in there until they send them back to Afghanistan. We've written letters from school, to the prime minister, to the queen, to lots of people, asking them to let Aman stay. They don't even bother to write back. And I've written to Aman too, lots of times. He wrote back only once, just after he got there, saying that one of the worst things about being locked up in his prison place is that he can't go out at night and look at the stars."

"Prison place? What d'you mean, prison place?" Grandpa asked.

"Yarl's—something or other," I said, trying to picture the address I'd written to. Then it came to me. "Yarl's Wood, that's it."

"That's near here, I know it is. Not far anyway," said Grandpa. "Maybe you could visit him."

"It's no good. They don't let kids in," I said. "We asked. Mum rang up, and they said it wasn't allowed. I was too young. And anyway, I don't even know if he's still in there. Like I said, he hasn't written back for a while now."

Grandpa and I didn't talk for some time. We were just stargazing again, and that was when I first had the idea. Sometimes I think that's where the idea must have come from. The stars.

"AND THEY KEEP KIDS IN THERE?"

Matt

I was worried about how Grandpa might react, but it was worth a try, I thought.

"Grandpa?" I said. "I've been thinking about Aman. I mean, maybe we could find out. Maybe you could ring up, or something, and find out if he's still there. And if he is, then you could go, Grandpa. You could go and see Aman instead of me, couldn't you?"

"But I hardly know him, do I?" Grandpa replied. "What would I say?"

I could tell he didn't much like the idea. So I didn't push it. You couldn't push Grandpa, everyone in the family knew that. As Mum often said, he could be a stubborn old cuss. So we sat there in silence, but all the time I knew he was thinking it over.

Grandpa said nothing more about it that night, nor at breakfast the next morning. I thought that either he'd forgotten all about it, or he'd already made up his mind he didn't want to do it. Either way, I didn't feel I could mention it again. And anyway, by now I think I had almost given up on the idea myself.

It was part of Grandpa's daily routine, whatever the weather, to get up early and take Dog for a walk along the river meadows to Grantchester—his "constitutional," he called it. And I know he always liked me to come with him when I was staying. I didn't much like getting up early, but once I was out there, I loved the walks, especially on misty mornings like this one.

There was no one around, except a rowing boat or two, and ducks, lots of ducks. There were cows in the meadows, so I had to keep Dog on the lead. I was having a bit of a struggle hanging on to him. There was always some rabbit hole he just *had* to stay behind to investigate, or some molehill he insisted he must make friends with. He was pulling all the time.

"Funny coincidence though," Grandpa said suddenly.

"What is?" I asked.

"That Yarl's Wood place you were talking about last night. I think that could be the detention center place Grandma used to visit, before she got ill. My memory's not what it was, but I think it was called Yarl's Wood—that's probably how I knew about it. She was a sort of befriender there."

"A befriender?"

"Yes," Grandpa said. "She'd go in and talk to the people in there—you know, the asylum seekers—to cheer them up a bit, because they were going through hard times. She did that a lot in prisons all her life. But she never said much about it, said it upset her too much to talk about it. Once a week or so, she'd go off and make someone a little happier for a while. She was like that. She always said I should do it too, that I'd be good at it. But I never had her courage. It's the idea of being locked up, I suppose, even if you know you can leave whenever you want to. How silly is that?"

"Do you know what Aman wrote in his letter, Grandpa?" I said. "He told me there's six locked doors and a barbed wire fence between him and the world outside. He counted them."

That was the moment we turned and looked at each other, and I knew then Grandpa had made up his mind he was going to do it. We never got to Grantchester. We turned around at once and went home, and Dog did not like that one bit.

Grandpa had been a journalist before he retired, so he knew how to find out about these things. As soon as we got back into the house, he was on the phone. He discovered that in order to visit Mrs. Khan and Aman in Yarl's Wood, he had to write a formal letter asking permission. It took a few days before the reply came back.

The good news was that they were still there, and the people at Yarl's Wood said that Grandpa could come on Wednesday, in two days' time it was, and that visiting times were between two and five in the afternoon. I wrote Aman a letter at once, telling him Grandpa was coming to visit him. I hoped he'd write back or phone. But he didn't, and I couldn't understand that at all.

All the way there I could see Grandpa was a bit nervous. He kept saying how he wished he had never agreed to do it in the first place. Dog was in the backseat, leaning his head on Grandpa's shoulder, watching the road in front as he always did. "I think Dog would drive this car himself if you let him," I said, trying to cheer Grandpa up a bit.

"I wish you could come in with me, Matt," he said.

"Me too," I told him. "But you'll be fine, Grandpa. Just go for it. And you'll like Aman. He'll remember you, I know he will. And you've got the Monopoly, haven't you? He'll beat you, Grandpa. But don't worry about that. He beats everyone. And tell him to write to me, will you? Or text, or phone?"

We were driving up a long straight hill. It seemed to lead to nowhere but the sky. Only when we reached the top of the rise did we see the gates, and then the barbed wire fence all around.

"And they keep kids in there?" Grandpa breathed.

WE WANT YOU BACK

Grandpa

I left Matt and Dog in the car and walked up toward the gates. I wasn't looking forward to this at all. I had that same sinking feeling in the pit of my stomach that I remember from my first day at school.

An unsmiling security guard was opening the gate. He suited the place. If Matt hadn't been there watching me from the car as I knew he must be, I'd have turned around at that point, got back in the car and gone home. But I couldn't shame myself, I couldn't let him down.

I turned around and saw that Matt was already out of the car and taking Dog for a walk, as he'd said he would. We gave each other a wave, and then

I was inside the gates. There was no going back now.

As I walked down the road toward the detention center building, I tried to keep my courage up by thinking about Matt. Ever since I'd been on my own these last two years, Matt had been to stay a lot. I loved to watch him playing with Dog.

Dog was getting on these days, like me, but he was like a puppy when Matt came. Matt kept him young, kept me young too. I only had to think of them both together, and they'd make me smile. They'd cheer me up. And that was good for me. I'd been rather down in the dumps just recently. Matt and I, we weren't just grandfather and grandson anymore; we'd become the best of friends.

But as I joined some other visitors making their way in, I was wondering what was the point of visiting Aman. After all, weren't these asylum seekers at Yarl's Wood about to be deported and sent back to where they'd come from anyway? So what was the point of visiting? I mean, what could I do? What could I say that could make any difference?

But Matt wanted me to do it for Aman. So there I was, inside the place now, doors locking behind me, the Monopoly set under my arm. I could hear the sound of children crying.

Like all the other visitors, I was being processed. The Monopoly set had to be handed over to be checked by security, and I got a stern telling-off for bringing it with me in the first place. It was against the rules, but they might bring it in later, they said grudgingly.

Everywhere there were more of those unsmiling security guards. The pat-down search was done brusquely and in hostile silence. Everything about the place seemed to me to be hateful: the bleak locker room where visitors had to leave their coats and bags, the institutional smell, the sound of keys turning in locks, the sad plastic flowers in the visitors' meeting room and always the sound of some child crying.

Then I saw them, the only ones still without a visitor. I recognized Aman at once, and I could tell he knew me too, as Matt had said he would. Aman and his mother were sitting there at the table, waiting for me, looking up at me, vacantly. There were no smiles. Neither of them seemed that pleased to see me. It was all too set up, too formal, too stiff.

Like everyone else in the room, we had to sit facing one another on either side of a table. And there were officers everywhere, in their black-and-white uniforms, keys dangling from their belts, watching us.

Aman's mother sat there, shoulders slumped, stone-faced, sad and silent. She had deep dark rings under her eyes and seemed locked inside herself. As for Aman, he was even smaller than I remembered him and pinched and thin like a whippet. His eyes were pools of loneliness and despair.

I kept trying to tell myself, don't pity them. They don't want that, they don't need that, and they'll know it at once if you do. They're not victims, they're people. Try to find something in common. Do what Matt said in the car. Just go for it. And pray the Monopoly arrives.

"How is Matt?" Aman said.

"He's outside," I told him. "They won't let him in."

Aman smiled wanly at that. "Strange," he said. "We want to get out, but they won't let us. And he wants to get in, but they won't let him."

I tried, again and again, to make some small

16

talk with his mother. The trouble was that she spoke very little English, so Aman always had to translate for her. Aman only became animated at all, I noticed, when we talked about Matt, and even then I found myself asking all the questions. I think we'd have all sat there in silence if I hadn't. Any question not about Matt, he'd just divert to his mother and translate her replies, which were mostly "yes" or "no." However hard I tried, I just could not seem to get a proper conversation going among the three of us.

So when Aman spoke up for himself suddenly, I was taken a little by surprise. "My mother is not well," he said. "She had one of her panic attacks this morning. The doctor gave her some medicine, and this makes her quite sleepy." He spoke very correctly and with hardly a trace of an accent.

"Why did she have a panic attack?" I asked, regretting my question at once. It seemed too intrusive, too personal.

"It is this place. It is being shut in here," he replied. "She was in prison once in Afghanistan. She does not talk about it much. But I know they beat her. The police. She hates the police. She hates to be locked in. She has bad dreams of the prison in Afghanistan, you understand? So sometimes when she wakes up in here, and she sees she is in prison again, and she sees the guards, she has a panic attack."

That was when the security guard suddenly arrived with the Monopoly game.

"You're lucky," he said. "Just this once, right?" And he walked away.

Miserable git, I thought. But I knew it was best to keep my feelings to myself. Now that I'd gotten it, I didn't want him to take it away.

"Monopoly," I said. "Matt says you like it, that you play quite well."

His whole face lit up. "Monopoly!" he said. " Look, Mother, Monopoly. You remember where we played it first?" Then he turned to me. "I used to play it a lot with Matt. I never lose," he said. "Never."

He opened the board at once and set it all up, rubbing his hands with delight when it was done. Then he started to laugh and couldn't seem to stop. "You see what it says here?" he cried, his finger stabbing at the board. "It says, 'go to jail.' Go to jail! That is very funny, isn't it? If I land here I will go to jail, in a jail. And so will you!"

His laughter was infectious, and very soon the two of us were almost hysterical.

That was when I saw another officer coming over toward us, a woman this time, but no less officious. "You're disturbing people. Keep it down," she said. "I won't tell you again. Any more of that and I'll end the visit, understand?"

She was being unnecessarily offensive and I did not like it one bit. This time, I did not try to hide my feelings. "So we're not allowed to laugh in here, is that right?" I protested. "People can cry, but they can't laugh, is that it?"

The officer gave me a long, hard look, but in the end she just turned around and walked away. It was a little victory, but I could see from the smile on Aman's face that he thought it was a lot more than that.

"Nice one," he whispered, giving me a secretive thumbs-up.

SHADOW

Grandpa

Matt had been right about Aman's prowess at Monopoly. Within an hour he owned just about all of London, and had left me bankrupt and in jail.

"You see?" he said, punching the air with both fists in triumph. "I am very good in business, like my father was. He was a farmer. Where we used to live in Bamiyan, in Afghanistan. He had sheep, many sheep, the best sheep in the valley. And he grew apples too, big green ones. I love apples."

"I've got some nice ones in my garden at home," I told him. "Lovely pink ones. James Grieve, they're called. I'll bring you some next time I come."

"They won't let you," he said ruefully.

"I can try," I told him. "I got the Monopoly game in, didn't I?"

He smiled at that. Then, leaning forward suddenly and ignoring his mother, he began asking me all sorts of questions, some about where I lived, what job I did, about what football team I supported— I could tell that Matt had told him a fair bit about me already and that pleased me a lot. But Aman wanted to talk mostly about Matt, about how he'd gotten all his letters, and how after a while he decided he couldn't write back, because he knew he wouldn't be seeing Matt again and it only made him sad.

"You mustn't say that," I told him. "You don't know you won't be seeing him again."

"Yes, I do," he said. I knew he was right, of course, but I suppose I thought I should give him some hope.

"You never know," I said. "You never know."

It was then that I remembered the family photo I'd brought in with me from home, at the last moment—another of Matt's ideas, and a good one too, I'd thought. I took it out of my jacket pocket and was about to hand it over.

Suddenly there was a guard yelling at us. Then she was striding across the room to our table—the same woman who had told me off before. Everyone in the room was looking at us now. "It's not allowed!" She was standing right over us by now, still shouting. "Are you just trying to make a nuisance of yourself, or what?"

Now I was properly angry, and I let her know it. "For goodness' sake, it's just a family photo." I held it up to show her. "Look," I said. She took it from me and examined it sullenly, taking her time before giving it back to me.

"In the future," she told me, "everything has to be passed by security. Everything."

I just nodded, buttoning my lip till she'd gone. I hated myself for doing it, for not arguing back. But I knew that to have a stand-up row with her would be pointless—if I wanted Aman to see the photo. I waited till she'd gone away, winked triumphantly at Aman, slid the photo across the table and then began pointing out who everyone was. "That's the family in the garden, last summer. There's the apple tree. And that's Matt there, kneeling down beside Dog. Yes, I know. Not a very imaginative name for a dog, is it? I think he must be about the same age as Matt, same age as you. That's pretty old for a dog."

A sudden frown came over Aman's face. He picked up the photo to look at it more closely. "Shadow," he murmured, and I saw his eyes were filling with tears. "Shadow."

"I'm sorry?" I said, not understanding at all. "Is it something in the photo?"

Without any warning, Aman got up and rushed out of the room. His mother went after him at once, leaving me sitting there and feeling rather stupid. I looked down at the photo, still trying to work out what there could possibly be in this family snap-shot that had upset him so much.

That was when another officer came wandering over and spoke to me, in a low and overly confiding tone. "Temperamental, you see," he said. "That's the trouble with them. And I'm warning you, that one can be a bit surly too."

I felt like getting up and shaking him. I should have given him a piece of my mind. I should have said, "And how would you feel being caged up in here like this? He's just a kid, with no home, no hope, nothing to look forward to, except deportation."

Instead, and for the second time that day, I said nothing. In keeping silent as I had, I felt I had betrayed Aman yet again. Whatever way I looked at it, the whole thing had all been my fault. I should never have shown Aman the photo.

He was just beginning to trust me and I'd blown it. I didn't understand why, but that didn't make me feel any better about it. People were looking at me from all around the room. I was sure they thought I had upset Aman intentionally somehow. I waited for a few minutes, hoping he might come back, but longing at the same time to get out of there. When he didn't reappear, I decided to pack up the Monopoly game as quickly as I could and go.

I had just collected up the last of the Monopoly money and was closing the lid, when I saw Aman coming back across the room toward me. He sat down opposite me again, without speaking a word, without even looking at me. I thought I'd better say something.

"I can leave the Monopoly game, if you'd like, if they'll let me," I said. "You can play it with your friends maybe."

"I don't have any friends in here," he said, still not lifting his eyes. "All my friends I had are on the outside. I'm on the inside." Then he did look up at me. "I've got a photo of my friends though. Mother says I should show you."

He was looking around the room, making quite sure no one was looking. Then he took a piece of folded paper out of his pocket and handed it to me surreptitiously under the table. I opened it out on my knee.

It was an e-mail printout of a photo of a school football team, in blue uniforms. They were all crowding around one another and laughing into the camera. Matt was standing at the back, his arms raised in the air, as if he had just scored a goal.

"That is my football team, and there is Matt. See him?" Aman said. "They sent it to me from school. And that's my shirt." They were holding up a bright blue football shirt. On the back was a number 7 and, underneath it in large letters, AMAN.

"If you count the players," he went on, "you will

see there are only ten of them. There should be eleven. I'm the one that is missing. That's Marlon, center forward, twenty-seven goals last year, as good as Rooney, better even. And the tall one, like a giraffe—next to Matt at the back—that's Flat Stanley, our goalie, the one grinning all over his face and giving me the thumbs-up? Can you see him?"

I could see him, right in the middle at the back. Along with all the others in the back row, he was holding up a huge banner that read WE WANT YOU BACK.

"These are my friends," Aman told me. "I want to go back to them, back to my school, back to my home in Manchester. It is where I belong, where Mother belongs. It is where Uncle Mir lives, where all our family lives. Mother says she is sorry, but she is very tired now, and she must lie down. But she said I must come back to see you, to talk to you. When I spoke to Mother just a few moments ago, she said that she had a dream about you last night, even before she met you, and about Father, and about the cave in Bamiyan where we lived, about the soldiers too, and Shadow."

"Shadow? What is . . . who is this Shadow?" I asked him.

"Shadow was our dog," said Aman. "He was just like the dog in your photo. We called her Shadow, when she was ours. And then later she was called Polly. She had two names, because she had two lives. She was brown and white, like yours. The same droopy eyes and long ears."

It was all too puzzling, too difficult too understand. "So Shadow," I said, "she's your dog, and she's back at your home in Manchester then? Is that right?"

Aman shook his head. "No. It's like Mother told me," he said. "She said I should tell you everything, all about Shadow, and about Bamiyan, and about how we came to be in this place. Like I said, Mother says she had a dream about you last night, before she even met you. And in the dream, she told me you took us by the hand and led us out of here. She says she was not sure about you at first, but now she is. She says you are a good listener with a kind heart, that all good friends are good listeners. Like Matt, she said, just like Matt. Why else would you come to see us if you did not want to listen? She says you are our last chance, our last hope of going home to Manchester, of staying in England. This is why she told me I must tell you the whole story now, right from the beginning, so you will know why we have come here to England and what has happened to us. She says that maybe you can help us, God willing. She says there is no one else who can, not now. Will you help us?"

"I will try, Aman, of course I will," I replied. "But I don't want to build up any false hopes. I really can't promise anything."

"I don't want promises," he said. "I just want you to listen to our story. That's all. Will you do that?"

"I'm listening," I told him.

BAMIYAN

Aman

I think you should know about my grandfather first, because in a way he was the beginning.

I didn't know him, but Mother often told me his stories—she still does sometimes—so, in a way, I do know him.

There was a time, so Grandfather told her, when Afghanistan was not as it is today. Bamiyan, where we lived, was a beautiful, peaceful valley. There was plenty to eat and the different peoples did not fight one another, Pashtun, Usbek, Tagik, Hazara—my family is from the Hazara people.

Then the foreigners came, the Russians first, with their tanks and their planes, and after that, there was no more peace, and soon there was no more food. My grandfather fought against them with the Mujahadin resistance fighters. But the Russian tanks came to our valley, to Bamiyan, and killed him, and many others.

All this was long before I was born.

After the Russians were driven out, Mother remembers that everyone was happy for a while. But then the Taliban fighters came in after them. At first everyone liked them, because they were Muslims like us. But we soon learned what they were really like. They hated us, especially Hazara people like us. They wanted us dead. If you did not agree with them, they killed you. They left us with nothing. They destroyed everything. They burned our fields. They blew up all our homes, every one of them. They killed whoever they wanted to. There was nothing anyone could do, except hide.

That is why I was born in a cave in the cliff face above the village. I grew up in this cave, with my mother and grandmother. I wasn't unhappy. I went to school. I had friends to play with. I knew nothing different.

Mother and Grandmother argued a lot, mostly about the same thing, about Grandmother's jewels, which she kept hidden away, sewn into her mattress. Mother was always trying to get her to sell them, to buy food when we were hungry. And Grandmother always refused. She said we were always hungry, and that we would manage to survive somehow, God willing. She would always say that there was something more precious even than food, and she was saving her jewels for that. She would not say what this was and that always made Mother very angry and upset. But I did not mind them arguing that much. I was used to it, I suppose.

Everyone I cared about in the world lived in these caves, a hundred or more of us, because there was nowhere else to go, because the Taliban had left us nowhere else to live. They had blown up all of Bamiyan, all of the houses, even the mosque.

And they did more than that. They blew up also the great stone statues of the Buddha that had been carved out of the cliff face thousands of years before. Mother watched them do it. She told me they were the biggest stone sculptures in the whole world and that people from far away used to come to Bamiyan to see them because they were so famous. But there is nothing left of them now, just great piles of stones. The Taliban blew up our whole lives.

They were cruel people.

Then the Americans came with their tanks and their helicopters and their planes, and the Taliban were driven out of the valley, most of them anyway. We all thought things would be better for us from now on. Father spoke a little English, so he became like an interpreter for the Americans. People kept saying there would soon be new houses for us to live in and a new school. But nothing seemed to change. There was some more food now, but never enough. So we were still hungry. In the cave Mother and Grandmother started quarreling again.

Things were getting back to normal.

But then one night the Taliban came to our cave and they took my father away. I was six years old. They called him a traitor because he had helped the infidel Americans. Mother fought them, but she wasn't strong enough. I screamed at them, but they just ignored me.

We never saw my father again. I remember him very well though. They cannot take away my memories of him. He used to show me the house down in the valley where he had lived, and we would sometimes walk the land where he used to graze his sheep and grow his onions and his melons, and the orchard where he grew his big green apples.

Father would always let me go with him to load up the donkey with sticks for the fire. And every day we would go down to the stream to fetch the water and carry it back up the steep hill to the cave. Sometimes he would take me into town to buy some bread, or a little meat from the butcher, if we had any money. Everyone liked him. We laughed a lot together and he would wrestle with me and play with me.

He was a good father. He was a good man.

But the Taliban had destroyed everything, cut down the orchards, burned the crops, took Father away. I never heard him laugh again. All we had left of him was his old donkey. I would talk to him instead sometimes. He was very sad, like me. I think maybe that donkey missed Father as much as I did.

After that there were just the three of us left in the cave, Mother, Grandmother and me. For months after Father was taken away, Grandmother would spend her days lying on the mattress in the corner and Mother would sit there beside her, gazing at nothing, hardly speaking. It was up to me now to find enough rice or bread to live on. I begged for it. I stole it. I had to. I fetched the water from the stream, a long walk down the hill and a long walk up, and I tried to bring in enough sticks to keep the fire going.

Somehow we managed to get through the winters without starving or freezing to death. But Grandmother's legs were getting worse all the time. She could hardly get up at all now unless one of us helped her.

What happened to Mother was my fault. I was with her at the market in town when I stole the apple, just one apple, nothing much—we had none left of our own by now. I was good at pinching things. I had never been spotted before. But this time I got careless. This time I got caught.

"DIRTY DOG! DIRTY FOREIGN DOG!"

Aman

I remember there was lots of shouting. "Filthy thief! Lousy beggar! Stop him! Stop him!" I tried to run away. But before I could escape, someone grabbed me. He kept hitting me and would not let go of me.

Mother came to my rescue, to protect me, but a crowd gathered and then suddenly the police were there. Mother told them it was her who stole the apple, not me. So they arrested Mother, instead of me, and took her off to prison. They beat her there. She still has the marks on her back. She was gone for nearly a week.

They tortured her.

When she came back she just lay on the mattress beside Grandmother and they cried together for days. She turned her face away from me and would not speak to me. I wondered if she would ever speak to me again.

It wasn't long after this that the dog first came to our cave—a dog just like your dog in that photo you showed me.

But when I saw her that first evening, she was thin and dirty and covered in sores. I was just crouching over the fire warming myself when I looked up and saw her sitting there, staring at me. She wasn't like any dog I had seen before—small, with short legs and long ears and nut-brown eyes.

I shouted at her to go away—you understand, we do not have dogs inside our homes in Afghanistan. Dogs have to live outside with the other animals. Of course, I have lived here a long time now and I know that in England it is different. Some people here like dogs better than they like children. Actually, I think if I was a dog, they would not shut me up in here like this.

So anyway, I threw a stone at this dog to shoo her away. But she stayed right where she was and would not move. She just sat there.

I saw then that she was shivering. You could

see her hip bones sticking out—she was that thin. She had sores all over her and you could tell she was starving. So instead of throwing another stone at her, I threw her a piece of stale bread. She snapped it up at once, chewed on it, swallowed it and then licked her lips, waiting for more.

I chucked her another piece. Then, before I knew it, she had come right into the cave and was lying down there beside me, close to the fire, making herself at home as if she belonged there. I noticed then that there was a wound on her leg, like she'd been in a dog fight or something. She kept worrying at it and licking it.

Mother and Grandmother were both fast asleep. I knew they'd chase the dog out as soon as they saw her there. But I liked her with me. I wanted her to stay. She had kind eyes, friendly eyes. I knew she wouldn't hurt me. So I lay down and slept beside her.

Early the next morning, she followed me down to the stream when I went to fetch the water. She was limping badly all the way. She let me bathe her leg and clean her wound. Then I told her she had to go and clapped my hands at her to try to drive her away. I knew that anyone seeing her might well throw stones at her—like I had, after all—and I didn't want that. But all the way back up the hill, she would not leave my side. Sure enough, as soon as we were spotted, a whole bunch of kids came running down the track and chased her off. They threw stones at her and shouted at her, "Dirty dog, dirty foreign dog!"

I tried all I could to stop them, but they wouldn't listen. I don't blame them now. After all, as I said, she did look different, not at all like the kind of dog any of us might have seen before. She scampered off and disappeared. I thought that was the last I'd ever see of her.

But that evening she turned up again at the mouth of the cave. I discovered then that she liked tripe, however rotten it was. You know tripe? It's a sort of meat, from the stomach lining of a cow—it was the only meat we could ever afford in Bamiyan. Anyway, there were a few rotten bits still left, so I threw her those.

But then later on, when the dog crept in to be by the fire again, Mother and Grandmother woke up and saw what was going on. They became very angry with me, and said all dogs were unclean, and that she shouldn't be allowed in. So I picked her up and put her down just outside the cave, where she sat and watched us, until Mother and Grandmother had gone to bed. She seemed to know it was safe to come in then, because when I lay down, she was right there beside me again.

"YOU MUST COME TO ENGLAND"

Aman

For weeks and weeks that's how it went on.

Somehow, the dog just seemed to know that when I was alone, or when they were fast asleep, it was all right for her to come inside the cave. And she knew when to keep her distance too. She'd be sitting there in the mouth of the cave when I woke every morning and she'd come with me down to the stream. She'd have a good long drink and wait for me to bathe the wound in her leg. Then, so long as there was no one else about, she would come with me when I went off with the donkey to gather sticks for the fire.

But there were some days, particularly when my friends were around a lot, that I'd hardly see her at all, just an occasional glimpse of her in the distance, watching me. I'd miss her then, but it was good to know she was still around. But sooner or later every evening she'd be there again at the mouth of the cave, waiting for her food, waiting for Mother and Grandmother to fall asleep. Then in she'd come, and she'd lie down beside me, her face so close to the fire that I thought she'd burn her whiskers.

One morning, I woke up early and found the dog was not there. And then I saw why. Grandmother was already awake. She was sitting up on the mattress, with Mother still lying down beside her, and I could see Mother was upset, almost in tears. I thought they'd had another quarrel maybe or that Mother's back was hurting her again.

But I soon learned what this was all about. They had talked about it often enough before, about the idea of Mother and me leaving Bamiyan, and going to England on our own, without Grandmother. She was far too old to come with us, she said. Grandmother would sometimes read out Uncle Mir's postcards from England. I had never even met Uncle Mir—he is Mother's older brother—but I felt as if

I had. I knew his story. He had left Bamiyan long before I was born.

Everyone in the caves knew about Uncle Mir, how he had gone off as a young man to find a job in Kabul, that he had met and married an English nurse, a girl called Mina, and then gone off with her to live in England. He had never come back, but he wrote often to Grandmother. Uncle Mir was her only son, so all his letters and postcards were very precious to her.

She was always taking them out and looking at them. They had been brought over to her from time to time by Uncle Mir's friends when they were visiting from England, and she'd kept them hidden in her mattress with all her other precious things. She loved to show me the postcards, of red buses, or of red-coated soldiers marching, of bridges over the river in London. There was one that she read to us, over and over again. I remember almost every word of it. Whenever she read it, it started an argument.

"One day," Grandmother would read out, "you must all come to England. You can live in our house. Mina and I have plenty of room for everyone. There is no war here, no fighting. My taxi business is good now. I have money I could send. I could help you to come."

And Mother would always argue. "I don't care about Mir and his postcards. And anyway, haven't I told you and told you? I'm not going anywhere without you. When your legs are better, God willing, then maybe."

"If you wait for my legs to get better, you will never go," Grandmother would argue back. "I am your mother. But your father would say the same if he was still with us. I am only asking you to do what I say, because it is what he would say. I am old. I have had my time. I know this. I feel it inside me. These legs will never walk again like they did. You and Aman must go. There is nothing for you in this place except hunger and cold and danger. You know what will happen if you stay. You know the police will come again. Go to England, to Mir. You will be safe there. He will look after you. There, you will be far from danger, far from the police. Listen to what Mir is telling us. There, the police will not put you in prison and beat you. There, you will not have to live in a cave like an animal."

Mother often tried to interrupt her and Grandmother hated that. One day, I remember, she became really angry, as angry as I had ever seen her.

"You should have some respect for your old mother," she cried. "You expect Aman to do as you say, don't you? Don't you? Well, now you must do as *I* say. I tell you, I will be in God's hands soon enough. I do not need you to stay. God will look after me, as he will look after you on your journey to England."

She reached in under her dress and brought out an envelope, which she emptied out onto the blanket beside her. I had never seen so much money in all my life. "Last week, Mir's friend came again with another card, and this time with some money too, enough, he says, to get you out of Afghanistan, through Iran, and Turkey, and all the way to England. And on the outside of the envelope here, he has written the phone numbers of people he says you must contact, in Kabul, in Teheran, in Istanbul. They will help you. And you must take these too."

She was taking off her necklace, pulling the rings from her fingers. "Take these, and I shall give you also all the jewels I have been keeping for you all this time. Sell them well in Kabul and they will help to buy you your freedom. They will take you away from all this fear and ignorance. It is fear and ignorance that kills people in their hearts, that makes them cruel. Take Father's donkey too. It's what he would have wanted. You can sell him, when you do not need him anymore. Do not argue with me. Take them, take the envelope and the money, take the jewels, take my beloved grandson and just go. And God willing, you will get to England safely."

In the end, Grandmother managed to persuade Mother that we should at least speak to Uncle Mir on the phone. So the next time we went into town, to the market, we phoned him from the public phone. Mother let me talk to him when she had finished. In my ear, Uncle Mir sounded very close by, I remember that. He talked to me in a very friendly way, as if he had known me all my life. Best of all, he told me he supported Manchester United, and that was my team. And he had even seen David Beckham, and my best hero too, Ryan Giggs! He said he'd take me to a match and that he'd let us stay with him and Mina as long as we needed to, until we could find a place of our own. After I talked to him, I was so excited. All I wanted to do was to go to England, go right away.

After the phone call, Mother stopped to buy some flour in the market and I walked on. When I turned around after a while, to see if she was coming, I saw one of the stallholders was shouting at her and waving his hands angrily. I thought it was an argument about money, that maybe she'd been shortchanged. They were always doing that in the market.

But it wasn't that.

She caught up to me and hurried me away. I could see the fear in her eyes. "Don't look around, Aman," she said. "I know this man. He is Taliban. He is very dangerous."

"Taliban?" I said. "Are they still here?" I thought the Taliban had been defeated long ago by the Americans and driven into the mountains. I couldn't understand what she was saying.

"The Taliban, they are still here, Aman," she said, and she could not stop herself from crying now. "They are everywhere, in the police, in the army, like wolves in sheep's clothing. Everyone knows who they are and everyone is too frightened to speak.

That man in the market, he was one of those who came to the cave and took your father away and killed him."

I turned around to look. I wanted to run back and tell him face-to-face he was a killer. I wanted to look him in the eye and accuse him. I wanted to show him I was not afraid. "Don't look," Mother said, dragging me on. "Don't do anything, Aman, please. You'll only make it worse."

She waited till we were safely out of town before telling me more. "He was cheating me in the market," she said, "and when I argued, he told me that if I do not leave the valley, he will tell his brother and he will have me taken to prison again. And I know his brother only too well. He was the police-man who put me in prison before. He was the one who beat me and tortured me. It wasn't because of the apple you stole, Aman. It was so that I would not tell anyone about what his brother had done to your father, so that I would not say he was Taliban. What can I do? I cannot leave Grandmother. She cannot look after herself. What can I do?" I held her hand to try to comfort her, but she cried all the way home.

I kept telling her it would be all right, that I would look after her.

That night I heard Mother and Grandmother whispering to each other in the cave and crying together too. When they finally went to sleep, the dog crept into the cave and lay down beside me. I buried my face in her fur and held her tight. "It will be all right, won't it?" I said to her.

But I knew it wasn't going to be. I knew something terrible was going to happen. I could feel it.

"WALK TALL, AMAN"

Aman

Early the next day the police came to the cave. Mother had gone down to the stream for water, so I was there alone with Grandmother when they came, three of them. The stallholder from the market was with them. They said they had come to search the place.

When Grandmother struggled to her feet and tried to stop them, they pushed her to the ground. Then they turned on me and started to beat me and kick me. That was when I saw the dog come bounding into the cave. She didn't hesitate. She leaped up at them, barking and snarling. But they lashed out at her with their feet and their sticks and drove her out.

After that they seemed to forget about me and

just broke everything they could in the cave, kicked our things all over the place, stamped on our cooking pot and one of them peed on the mattress before they left.

I didn't realize at first how badly Grandmother had been hurt, not till I rolled her over onto her back. Her eyes were closed. She was unconscious. She must have hit her head when she fell. There was a great cut across her forehead. I kept washing the blood away, kept trying to wake her. But the blood kept coming and she wouldn't open her eyes.

When Mother came back some time later, she did all she could to revive her, but it was no good. Grandmother died that evening. Sometimes I think she died because she just didn't want to wake up, because she knew it was the only way to make Mother and me leave, the only way to save us. So maybe Grandmother won her argument with Mother, in her own way, the only way she could.

We left Bamiyan the next day, the day Grandmother was buried. We did as Grandmother had told us. We took Father's donkey with us, to carry the few belongings we had, the cooking things, the blankets, and the mattress, with Grandmother's jewels and Uncle Mir's money hidden inside it. We took some bread and apples with us, gifts from our friends for the journey, and walked out of the valley. I tried not to look back, but I did. I could not help myself.

Because of everything that had happened, I think, I had almost forgotten about the dog, which hardly seems fair when I think about it. After all, only the day before, she had tried to save my life in the cave. Anyway, she just appeared, suddenly, from out of nowhere. She was just there, walking alongside us for a while, then running on ahead, as if she was leading us, as if she knew where she was going. Every now and then, she would stop, and start sniffing at the ground busily, then turn to look back at us. I wasn't sure whether it was to check that we were coming or to tell us everything was all right, that this was the road to Kabul, that all we had to do was follow her.

Mother and I took turns riding up on the donkey. We did not talk much. We were both too sad, about Grandmother's death, about leaving, and too tired as well. But to begin with the journey went well enough. We had plenty of food and water to keep us going. The donkey kept plodding on and the dog stayed with us, still going on ahead of us, nose to the ground, tail wagging wildly.

Mother said it was going to take us many days of walking to reach Kabul, but we managed to find shelter somewhere each night. People were kind to us and hospitable. The country people in Afghanistan haven't much, but what they have, they share.

At the end of each day's walk, we were always tired out. I wasn't exactly happy. I couldn't be. But I was excited. I knew I was setting out on the biggest adventure of my life. I was going to see the world beyond the mountains, like Uncle Mir.

I was going to England.

As we came closer to Kabul, the road was busier than it had been, with trucks and army vehicles and carts. The donkey was nervous in the traffic, so Mother and I were walking. Then we saw ahead of us the police checkpoint. I could tell at once that Mother was terrified. She reached for my hand, clutched it and did not let go. She kept telling me not to be frightened, that it would be all right, God willing. But I knew she was telling herself that more than she was telling me.

As we reached the barrier the police started shouting at the dog, swearing at her, then throwing stones at her. One of the stones hit her, and she ran off, yelping in pain. That made me really angry, angry enough to be brave. I found myself swearing back at them, and telling them exactly what I thought of them, what everyone thought of the police. They were all around us then, like angry bees, shouting at us, calling us filthy Hazara dogs, threatening us with their rifles.

Then—and I couldn't believe it at first—the dog came back. She was so brave. She just went for them, snarling and barking, and she managed to bite one of them on the leg too, before they kicked her away. Then they were shooting at her. This time when she ran away, she did not come back. After that, they took us off behind their hut, pushed us up against the wall and demanded to see our ID papers. I thought they were going to shoot us, they were that angry.

They told Mother our papers were like us, no

good, that we couldn't have them back unless we handed over our money. Mother refused. So they searched us both, roughly, and disrespectfully too. They found nothing, of course.

But then they searched the mattress.

They cut it open and found the money and Grandmother's jewelry. The policemen shared out Uncle Mir's money and Grandmother's jewelry there and then, right in front of our eyes. They took what food we had left and even our water.

One of them, the officer in charge I think he was, handed me back the empty envelope and our papers. Then, with a sarcastic grin all over his horrible face, he dropped a couple of coins into my hand. "You see how generous we are," he said. "Even if you are Hazara, we wouldn't want you to starve, would we?"

Before we left, they decided to take Father's donkey too. All we had in the world as we walked away from that checkpoint, with their laughter and their jeering ringing in our ears, were a couple of coins and the clothes we stood up in. Mother's hand grasped mine tightly. "Walk tall, Aman. Do not bow your head," she said. "We are Hazara. We will not cry. We will not let them see us cry. God will look after us."

We both held back our tears. I was proud of her for doing that and I was proud of me too.

An hour or so later we were sitting there by the side of the road. Now there was no one watching, Mother had given herself up to tears. She was wailing and crying, her head in her hands. She seemed to have lost all heart, all hope. I think I was too angry to cry. I was nursing a blister on my heel, I remember, when I looked up and saw the dog come running toward us out of the desert. She leaped all over me, and then all over Mother too, wagging everything.

To my surprise, Mother did not seem to mind at all. In fact, she was laughing now through her tears. "At least," said Mother, "at least, we have one friend left in this world. She has great courage, this dog. I was wrong about her. I think maybe this dog is not like other dogs. She may be a stranger, but as such we should welcome her and look after her. She may be a dog, but I think she is more like a friend than a dog, like a friendly shadow that does not want to leave us. You never lose your shadow."

"That is what we should call her then," I told her. "Shadow. We'll call her Shadow." The dog seemed pleased with that as she looked up at me. She was smiling. She was really smiling. Soon she was bounding on ahead of us, sniffing along the road ahead of us, her tail waving us on.

It was strange. We had just lost all we had in the world, and only minutes before everything had seemed completely hopeless, but now that waving tail of hers gave us new hope. And I could see Mother felt the same. I knew at that moment that somehow we were going to find a way to get to England. Shadow was going to get us there. I had no idea how. But together, we were going to do it. Somehow, somehow.

SOMEHOW, SOMEHOW

Aman

We had to sit there for a long while, until it was dark. We had only the stars for company. Every truck that went by covered us in dust. But we got a lift in the end, in the back of a pickup truck full of melons, hundreds of them.

We were so hungry by now that we ate several of them between us, chucking the melon skins out of the back as we went along so that the driver wouldn't find out. Then we slept. It wasn't comfortable. But we were too tired to care. It was morning before we reached Kabul.

Mother had never in her life been to Kabul and neither had I. We were pinning all our hopes now on the contact telephone numbers Uncle Mir had written on the back of that envelope.

The first on his list was in Kabul, so the first thing we had to do was to look for a public phone. The driver dropped us off in the marketplace. It was the first time in my life I had ever been in a city. There were so many people, so many streets and shops and buildings, so many cars and trucks and carts and bicycles, and there were police and soldiers everywhere. They all had rifles, but there was nothing new or frightening for me about that. Everyone back home in Bamiyan had rifles too. I think just about every man in Afghanistan has a rifle. It was their eyes I was frightened of. Every policeman or soldier seemed to be looking right at us and only at us as we passed.

But then I did notice that it wasn't us they were interested in so much. It was Shadow. She was skulking along beside us, much closer to us than usual, her nose touching my leg from time to time. I could tell she wasn't liking all the noise and bustle of the place any more than we were.

It took a while to find a public phone. Mother arranged to meet Uncle Mir's contact and at first he was quite welcoming. He gave us a hot meal and

I thought everything was going to be fine now. But when Mother told him we had lost all the money Uncle Mir had sent us for the journey to England, that it had been stolen from us, he was suddenly no longer so friendly.

Mother pleaded with him to help. She told him we had nowhere to go, nowhere to spend the night. That was when I began to notice that like the police and the soldiers in the street, he too seemed to be more interested in Shadow than in us. He agreed then to let us have a room to stay in, but only for one night. It was a bare room except for a bed and a carpet, but after living my whole life in a cave, this was like a palace to me.

All we wanted was to sleep, but this man hung around and wouldn't leave us alone. He kept asking questions about Shadow, about where we had gotten her from, about what sort of dog she was. "This dog," he said, "she is a foreign-looking dog, I think. Does she bite? Is she a good guard dog?"

The more I saw of this man, the more I did not trust him. Shadow didn't much like him either and kept her distance. He had darting eyes and a mean and treacherous look about him. That's why I said what I did. "Yes, she bites," I told him. "And if anyone attacks us, she goes mad, like a wolf."

"A good fighter then?" he asked.

"The best," I said. "Once she bites, she never lets go."

"Good, that's good," he said. The man thought for a moment or two, never taking his eye off Shadow. "Tell you what, I'll do you a deal," he went on. "You give me the dog and I'll arrange everything for you. I'll give you enough money to get you over the border into Iran and all the way to Turkey. You won't have to worry yourselves about anything. How's that?"

It was Mother who understood at once what this man was after. "You want her for a fighting dog, don't you?" she asked him.

"That's right," he told her. "She's a bit on the small side. And a proper Afghan fighting dog will tear a foreign dog like her to bits. But so long as she puts up a good fight, that's all that counts. It's not just about size. It's the show they come to see. Have we got a deal?"

"No, no deal. We are not selling her, are we,

Aman?" Mother replied, crouching down and putting her arm around Shadow. "Not for anything. She's stuck by us and we're going to stick by her."

That's when the man lost his temper. He started yelling at us. "Who do you think you are? You Hazara, you're all the same, so high and mighty. You'd better think about it. You sell me that dog, or else! I'll be back in the morning."

He slammed the door behind him as he left and we heard the key turn in the lock. When I tried the door moments later, it wouldn't budge. We were prisoners.

COUNTING THE STARS

Aman

The window was high up, but Mother thought if we turned the bed on its side and climbed up, we might just be able to get out. So that's what we did. It was a small window, and there'd be a big drop on the other side, but we had no choice, we had to try. It was our only hope.

I went first, and Mother handed Shadow up to me. I dropped Shadow to the ground, saw her land safely and then followed her. It was more difficult for Mother, and it took some time, but in the end she managed to squeeze herself out of the window and jump down.

We were in an alleyway. No one was about. I wanted us to run, but Mother said that would attract attention. So we walked out of the alley and into the crowded streets of Kabul.

With lots of other people about, I thought we were safe enough, but Mother said we'd be better off out of Kabul altogether, as far away from that man as we could get. We had no money for food, no money for a bus fare. So we started walking, Shadow leading the way again. We just followed her through the city streets, weaving our way through the bustle of people and traffic, too exhausted to care which way she was taking us. North, south, east or west, it really did not bother us. We were leaving danger behind us and that was all that mattered.

By the time it got dark, we were already well outside the city. The stars and the moon were out over the mountains, but it was a cold night, and we knew we'd have to find shelter soon.

We had been trying to hitch a ride for hours, but nothing had stopped. Then we got lucky. A truck was parked up ahead of us, at the side of the road. I knocked on the window of the cab and asked the driver if we could have a ride. He asked where we came from. When I told him we were from

Bamiyan and we were going to England, he laughed and told us he was from a village down the valley, that he was Hazara like us. He wasn't going as far as England, only to Kandahar, and was happy to take us if that would help. Mother said we would go wherever he was going, that we were hungry and tired, and just needed to rest.

He turned out to be the kindest man we could have hoped to meet. He gave us water to drink and shared his supper with us. In the warm air of his cab, we soon shivered the cold out of us. He asked us a few questions, mostly about Shadow. He said he had only once before seen a foreign-looking dog like that, with the American soldiers or the British, he wasn't sure which.

"They use dogs like this to find the roadside bombs, to sniff them out," he said, shaking his head sadly. "Those soldiers, the foreign soldiers, they all look much the same in their helmets and some of them are so young. Just boys most of them, far from home, and too young to die." After that he stopped talking and just hummed along with the music on his radio. We were asleep before we knew it.

I don't know how many hours later, the driver

woke us up. "Kandahar," he said. He pointed out the way to the Iranian frontier on his map. "South and west. But you'll need papers to get across. The Iranians are very strict. Have you got any papers? You haven't, have you? Money?"

"No," Mother told him.

"Papers I can't help you with," the driver said. "But I have a little money. It's not much, but you are Hazara, you are like family, and your need is greater than mine."

Mother didn't like to take it, but he insisted. So thanks to this stranger, we were at least able to eat and to find a room to stay while we worked out what to do and where to go next. I don't know how much money the driver gave us, but I do know that by the time Mother had paid for the meal and the room for the night, there was very little left, enough only to buy us the bus fare out of town the next morning. But as it turned out, that didn't get us very far.

The bus that we had taken, that was supposed to take us all the way to the frontier, broke down out in the middle of the countryside, but it was now a countryside very different from the gentle valley of Bamiyan that I was used to. There were no orchards, no fields here, just desert and rocks as far as you could see, so hot and dusty by day that you could hardly breathe; and cold at night, sometimes too cold to sleep.

But there were always the stars. Father used to tell me you only had to try counting the stars and you always went to sleep in the end. He was right most nights. Night or day we were always thirsty, always hungry. And the blister on my heel was getting a lot worse all the time, and was hurting me more and more.

After walking for many days—I don't know how many—we came at last to a small village, where we had a drink from the well and rested for a bit while Mother bathed my foot. The people there stood at their doors and looked at us warily, almost as if we were from outer space.

When Mother asked the way to the frontier, they shrugged and turned away. Again it was Shadow that seemed to interest them, not us, and she was doing what she always did, running around, exploring everywhere with her nose. As we left I saw that some of the children were following us, watching us from a distance. Just outside the village we saw a crossroads ahead of us. "Now what?" I asked Mother. "Which way?"

That was when I noticed that Shadow had suddenly stopped. She was standing stock-still at the crossroads, head down, staring at the ground at the side of the road. I called out to her and she didn't even turn around. I knew something was wrong right away.

I looked behind me. The village children had stopped too, and one or two of them were pointing, not at Shadow, but at something farther away, farther down the road.

I saw then what they had seen, foreign soldiers, several of them, coming slowly toward us. The one in front had a detector—I'd seen them before in Bamiyan—and I knew what they were for. He was sweeping the road ahead of him for bombs. I think it was only then that I put two and two together, and realized what Shadow was doing. She had discovered a bomb. She was pointing to it. She was showing us. And I knew somehow that she was showing the soldiers too.

But they still couldn't see her. She was hidden from them by a boulder at the side of the road. So I just ran. I never even thought about it. I just ran, toward the soldiers, toward Shadow, toward the bomb.

POLLY

Aman

I was running and running, waving at the soldiers to warn them, screaming and yelling at them that there was a bomb, pointing to where it was, to where Shadow was.

All the soldiers had stopped by now and were crouching down, taking aim at me.

At that moment the whole world seemed to be standing still. I remember one of the soldiers standing up and shouting at me to stop where I was. I didn't understand any English then, of course, but he was making it quite clear what he wanted me to do. He was telling me to move back and to do it fast.

So I did.

I backed away till I found Mother's arms around me, holding me. She was sobbing with terror and it was only then that I began to be frightened myself, to realize at all how much danger we were in.

The soldier was walking now toward Shadow, calling out one word over and over again, but not to us, to Shadow. "Polly? Polly? Polly?"

Shadow turned, looked at him, wagged her tail just once and then she was back to being a statue again, head down, nose pointing. Shadow never wagged her tail at anyone unless it was a friend. She knew this soldier and he knew her.

They were old friends. They had to be.

But how could they be? I couldn't work it out at all. It was a weird moment. I knew the bomb might go off at any time, but all I could think about was how that soldier and Shadow could possibly have known each other.

The soldier was still shouting at us to move farther away, then waving at us to get down. Mother was pulling me backward all the time, almost dragging me, until I found myself lying down with her in the bottom of a ditch. Her arm was tight around me, her hand on top of my head, holding me down.

"Don't move, Aman," she whispered in my ear.

"Don't move." All the time we were lying there she did not stop praying.

I don't know how long we were lying there in the ditch for, only that I was wet through and through and that my foot was throbbing with pain. All the time I wanted to get up on my knees and have a look at what was going on, but Mother wouldn't let me.

We could hear the soldiers talking, but had no idea what was happening until we heard footsteps coming toward us along the road. We looked up to see two soldiers standing over us, one of them a foreigner, one in an Afghan uniform. Shadow was there too, panting hard, and looking very pleased with herself. The two soldiers helped us up out of the ditch and Shadow jumped up and down at us, greeting us as if she hadn't seen us for a month.

"It's all right," the Afghan soldier told us. "The bomb is safe now." He spoke in Pashto, but then at once repeated it in Dari. He seemed to know almost immediately that we were Hazara, that we spoke Dari.

The foreign soldier was shaking Mother's hand, then mine, and he was talking excitedly all the time, the Afghan soldier interpreting for him. "This is Sergeant Brodie. He's with the British army. He says you were very brave to do what you did. You may have saved many lives today and he wants to thank you. He wants to tell you something else too, about the dog. He couldn't believe his eyes when he first saw this dog, none of us could. He knew it was Polly at once. We all did. I knew it too. There's no other dog in the world like Polly. He says that Polly was always excited like this after she discovered a bomb. It's because she knows she has done her job well and it makes her really happy. But Sergeant Brodie wants to know how come she seems to know you so well?"

"Of course she knows me," I told them. "She's our dog, isn't she?"

They looked at each other, not seeming to understand what I was telling them.

"Your dog?" the British soldier asked me through the interpreter again. "I'm still trying to work this out. I mean, how long have you had her? Where did you find her?"

"Bamiyan," I said. "She came to our home. It was months ago, nearly a year maybe."

"*Bamiyan?*" The interpreter was amazed. They both were. "Sergeant Brodie says that is impossible," said the Afghan soldier. "Bamiyan is hundreds of miles away, up north. This whole thing is impossible."

As the interpreter was talking, the soldier seemed suddenly to be looking about him nervously. "Sergeant Brodie says we can't stand here chatting out in the open," the interpreter went on. "The Taliban could be watching us. They have eyes everywhere. They have ambushed us on this road before. But he has to find out more about all this, about you and Polly. We must go into the village, he says. We can be safer there."

So with Sergeant Brodie holding my hand, the soldiers behind us and Shadow running on ahead, showing us the way as usual, we walked back into the village, the village children all around us.

"QUITE A HERO"

Aman

So that's how we all found ourselves a few minutes later sitting inside a house in the village,
changed into dry clothes the villagers had found
for Mother and me and sipping glasses of tea, with
the whole room crowded with people, villagers
and soldiers, the interpreter and this Sergeant
Brodie, all of them listening, as I told them all about
how Shadow had wandered into our cave all those
months before, more than a year now, and how she'd
been hurt in the leg somehow and was starving,
how she'd gotten better and that we were now on
our way to England to live in Manchester, with our
uncle Mir, who had once shaken hands with Ryan
Giggs.

The soldiers laughed at that. It turned out that

one or two of them supported Manchester United and that Ryan Giggs was their hero too. So I knew then I was among friends.

All this time Shadow lay beside me, her head on my feet, eyeing everyone in the room.

When I had finished, Sergeant Brodie was the first to say anything. He spoke through his interpreter again.

"The sergeant says he's got something to tell you about this dog," he began. The interpreter spoke Dari with an accent I wasn't used to, but Mother and I understood enough. "He says you're going to find it difficult to believe this. He finds it difficult to believe it himself, but it really is true. He's asked all the soldiers who were here a year or so ago and they all agree. There is no doubt about it. We all know this dog. That dog, she is called Polly, and she's sniffed out more roadside bombs—the army calls them IEDs, improvised explosive devices— than any other dog in the whole army. Seventy-five. Today's was the seventy-sixth. And that dog disappeared, the sergeant says, about fourteen months ago now. He was there when it happened. And so was I.

"We were out on patrol, just like today. Sergeant Brodie was with us on that patrol too. He was Polly's handler. Polly lived with him and his family when they were back home in England. The sergeant was the one who trained her, looked after her and lived with her on the base. The best sniffer dog he'd ever known, he says. Everyone said so. Anyway, there we were, out on patrol, Sergeant Brodie and Polly going on ahead of us, checking the roadsides for bombs as usual. When we saw Polly was on to something, we all stopped. And that's when the Taliban ambushed us.

"The firefight that followed went on for an hour or so and when it was over we found we had one man wounded, Corporal Banford, it was, and Polly wasn't there. She was nowhere to be seen. She had disappeared. We called her and we called her, but we couldn't hang about looking for her. It was too dangerous.

"We called in a helicopter to get Corporal Banford out of there and off to hospital as quick as we could. Sadly, it wasn't quick enough. He died on the way to hospital. We came back to look for Polly the next day and told every patrol that went out after that to keep an eye out for her. But no one ever saw her again. So we all thought she'd been killed. We'd lost two soldiers that day. That's how we thought of her, as one of us."

The interpreter had to wait a few moments for the sergeant to begin again.

"Sergeant Brodie is saying," he went on, "that the Taliban target our sniffer dogs if they can— they know how valuable they are to us, how many soldiers' lives they save. That's what he thought had happened to her. That's what everyone thought. We put up a little memorial for her back at the base. Then, we come out here today, fourteen months later, and there you are waving us down to warn us, and there she is sniffing out a bomb just like she was when we last saw her. It's incredible. And if I've understood it right, that dog wandered hundreds of miles north, before she found you in Bamiyan, and then hundreds of miles back. I know it sounds silly, but I reckon she knew where she was going. She had to find someone to look after her, and that was you, and then she knew she had to come back where she belonged. Somehow she must have known the way home, sort of like a swallow does."

When he told me that last bit about Shadow knowing the way home, I was sure he had to be right. Wherever we had been since we left Bamiyan, Shadow always seemed to know the way to go. It was us, Mother and me, who had followed her, not the other way around. And so much else was making sense to me now, how Shadow was always running on ahead of us, nose to the ground, sniffing the roadside. This was what she'd been trained to do. She was an army sniffer dog, just like that driver in the truck had told us.

"Believe me, when they hear about this back at base," the interpreter said, "the sergeant says you are going to be quite a hero for our lads. After all, it was you who warned us about the bomb. And it was you who rescued Polly, looked after her and brought her back to us. They are going to be 'over the moon,' as they say in English—and so is his daughter back home in England. She loved that dog to bits. The whole family did, the sergeant himself most of all. Yes, you're going to be quite a hero."

SILVER, LIKE A STAR

Aman

As we set off again, Sergeant Brodie saw that I was limping and Mother told him through the interpreter about my bad foot. So I got a lift, a piggy-back ride, on Sergeant Brodie's back all the way to the base. No one had done that for me since Father died. It felt so good.

And the sergeant was right. At the base, they did make a real fuss of me, of all of us, particularly Shadow. Nothing was too much trouble. We slept in a warm bed, ate all we wanted, had a shower whenever we liked. And they had a doctor there too who had a look at my blister. She said it was infected, that I'd have to stay on the base for a while and not walk on it, not until it had healed up. They even let Mother telephone Uncle Mir in England.

So Mother and Shadow and me, we stayed there on the base—it must have been for nearly a week, I think. They gave us a little room of our own, and Mother slept a lot, and when my foot was better I played football with the soldiers.

That was when I first learned to play Monopoly too. It was Sergeant Brodie who taught me. I learned to say my first words in English and he learned some Dari too. Sergeant Brodie and me and Shadow, we'd spend a lot of time together, when he wasn't busy, when he wasn't out on patrol. Like all the other soldiers, he kept wanting to take photos of Shadow and me to send home on his phone.

Once, he showed me a live video of his daughter and his wife, taken on their phone. They were waving at me all the way from England and shouting "thank you" to me for saving Polly. I should have been happy, but I wasn't. There was something that was troubling me. And it was troubling Shadow too, I could tell.

I knew by now we'd have to be leaving soon, as soon as my heel was better, and somehow she seemed to know it too. As the days went by, Shadow wanted more and more to stay with us. But I could see she loved being with the soldiers too, particularly with Sergeant Brodie. He had even kept her favorite ball to remember her, the one she'd always liked to play with. The soldiers would throw it for her and she'd chase it right across the compound, bringing it back, but not letting it go, till she was given something to eat in return.

But she never played with them for too long. Always she came back to sit near me, and I'd catch her looking at me, and we'd both know what it was we were thinking. Is she Polly? Is she Shadow? Would she be coming with us when we left?

I knew the answer. She knew the answer. I think we both kept hoping that both of us were wrong. I could feel she was becoming theirs again, an army dog, Sergeant Brodie's dog. Polly, not Shadow. She still slept with us in our room, often came to lie down beside me with her head on my foot. I still hoped she would be coming with us, but I knew already deep down that it wasn't going to happen, that she would be staying on the base with the soldiers, that she was back with Sergeant Brodie where she belonged.

She knew it too, and was as sad about it as I

was, and as Mother was too—she often told me later that she could never have imagined that she could become so fond of a dog.

I think all the soldiers could see my sadness. The soldiers may have been exhausted when they came back into the base after a patrol, with their rifles and their helmets, but they always had a smile for me. They all knew by now why we were on the road, what we were running away from, all about how Mother had been treated by the police, about how Grandmother had died.

Sergeant Brodie came in to see us on the evening before we left, with the interpreter, who told us that the soldiers had collected some money to help us on our way, a "whip 'round," he called it. I think I knew what was coming next from the sad expression on his face. He said it all through the interpreter. He could hardly look at me.

"About Polly. I'm sorry, Aman, but she has to stay here. She's an army dog. Maybe you can come and see her again, when you get to England, I mean. How'd that be?" He was only trying to soften the blow, I realized that. But who knew if we would ever even make it to England, without Shadow to lead us there?

I cried when he'd gone out. I couldn't stop myself. Mother said it was for the best, that we'd be fine on our own from now on, God willing. And this time, she said, we were going to look after our money. That was why, with Shadow beside me on the bed, I spent most of our last night on the base hollowing out the heels of our shoes, the best place we could think to hide our money. Shadow watched me all the time. She knew for sure these would be our last few hours together.

I could hardly bear to look at her.

When we left the next morning, the soldiers were there to see us off and so was Shadow. Sergeant Brodie called for three cheers and when it was over he stepped forward to say good-bye to us. He pressed something into my hand. The interpreter was there to help him as usual. "Our regimental badge, Aman," he was telling me. "The sergeant says you've earned it. He says he hopes you get to England all right. And when you do, and if you ever need any help, let him know. He'll be there.

And if you want to see Polly again, just ask. You can always get in touch with him through the regiment. And he says to thank you, for bringing Polly back to him, for saving the lives of his men, that he'll never forget what you did for us, for all the lads, for the regiment."

I crouched down to say my last good-byes to Shadow, stroked the dome of her head and ruffled her ears. But I couldn't say anything. If I spoke, I knew I would cry, and I didn't want to do that, not in front of the soldiers.

As they drove us off the base, I longed for Shadow to jump up and come with us. But I knew she wouldn't, that she couldn't.

That was the last I saw of her.

They drove us to the nearest town and put us on a bus. I sat there clutching my badge. I looked down at it for the first time. It was silver, like a star, with what looked like a picture of castle walls on it. And there was some writing below that I couldn't read then.

(It said "Royal Anglian." I've still got it. I take it with me everywhere.)

We were on our way again, to England, to Uncle

Mir and Manchester. Sitting there on the bus, I remember I tried hard to think of Ryan Giggs, to stop me feeling so sad about leaving Shadow. But it didn't work. Then I looked down at my star, and squeezed it tight. It made me feel better. That silver star always has, ever since.

"THE WHOLE STORY, I NEED THE WHOLE STORY"

Grandpa

All this time, as Aman was telling his story, he had hardly looked up at me at all. It seemed to me that as he was telling it, he needed to relive his memories without any kind of distractions. He spoke so softly that he could almost have been talking to himself, his voice often barely a whisper. Sometimes I had to lean right forward to hear what he was saying. But throughout it all, his voice had been steady, until the very last bit, the moment he'd had to leave Shadow behind. I could hear then that he was fighting back the tears.

When he got up suddenly and rushed out of the

visiting room, I was sure it must be because he did not want me to see him crying. I knew too that he might not come back, that he might be too proud to have to face me again after that. But I waited there anyway, because somehow I felt there was at least a chance he would come back. After all, he'd come back the last time, hadn't he?

Sitting alone at the table, I wished more than anything that Matt could be with me. Aman wouldn't have run off like that if Matt had been there. They were friends, best friends. Matt would have been able to talk him around somehow.

It was then, with Aman's story still fresh in my head, that I first began to consider seriously whether there really might be something that could be done to help Aman and his mother—besides just visiting them, I mean.

The longer I sat there, and thought about the poverty of their lives in Bamiyan, of the suffering the whole family had lived through, of their determination to get out of Afghanistan and come to England, the more I hated to think of them locked up like criminals in this place. There was a terrible injustice going on here. Aman's story had awoken the journalist in me. I wanted to know more.

I wanted to know everything.

When Aman did come back a few minutes later, his mother was with him again. I hadn't expected this at all. There was so much I still had to find out about. I'd been hoping that when he came back, he would be able just to pick up his story where he'd left off. But I knew Aman was much more shy and reserved with his mother around, so I wasn't at all hopeful he would talk as easily or as freely as he had before. I could see his mother had been crying and was still very overwrought. She was rocking back and forth, clutching a handkerchief in both hands.

His mother spoke up then, but only to Aman, and in her own language. When she had finished, he translated for her. "Mother says she had to come and tell you herself that we cannot go back to Afghanistan, that the police would torture her again. She says the Taliban are not defeated, they are everywhere, in the police, everywhere. They will kill her, just like they killed Father. She says we have been living in England for six years now. This is our home. She says our lawyer cannot help us anymore, that the government won't even let us appeal. She has prayed to God that you will be able to help us. Her dream tells her you will, but she has come to ask you herself, to beg you to make her dream come true."

I didn't know what to say, only that I had to say something, and something encouraging too, but without making promises I could not keep.

"Tell her I can do my best, and I will," I told him. "But she must understand and so must you, Aman, that I am not a lawyer. I'm not sure what I can do, what anyone can do. But I do know that for me to be able to do anything at all, I will need you to tell me your whole story, from the time you left Shadow behind and got on the bus that day, until now, until today. I mean, how did you manage to get all the way to England? How have you been living and what exactly happened when they brought you in here? The more I know, the better. I need to know everything."

Aman talked to his mother for a few moments, to explain things. She was calmer now, more composed.

Then he turned back to me, took a deep breath and began his story again, reluctantly though, as if he did not want to remind himself at all of the rest of the story, as if he was dreading having to live through it again.

"GOD IS GOOD"

Aman

All right, if you think it will help, I'll go on then. The bus. We were on the bus. It was a comfortable bus, the most comfortable I'd ever been on. I was missing Shadow, of course I was; but apart from that, I was feeling really up. I think I imagined this bus would take us all the way to England. I was only eight then, remember. I hadn't any real idea where England was, nor how far away it was, nor how long it would take us to get there.

I think if we had known what a long and terrible journey it was going to be, then I'd never have gotten on that bus in the first place. As it turned out, that bus journey was the last time we were going to be comfortable, or happy, for a very long time.

Mother was sick with worry when we came to the frontier with Iran, I could see that. She told me we were going to play a game. We had to pretend we were asleep, if the soldiers came on board to check us. So that's what we did. I heard them coming down the bus, but they passed by us without stopping. I only dared to open my eyes when the bus was on its way again. We were through.

"You see, Aman," she whispered to me, "God is good. God is helping us."

She told me then that she had telephoned from the army base to Uncle Mir's contact in Teheran, the next big city, and he would be there waiting to meet us when we arrived, that he would take care of everything. So we had nothing more to worry about. I think I must have slept almost all the way, because I don't remember much about that journey, only that it seemed endless.

Uncle Mir's friend was there to meet us, as Mother had said. He walked us through the streets, warning us not to talk to anyone and not to look anyone in the eye, particularly policemen. He told us that if we got caught they would put us in prison or send us back to Afghanistan. So of course we did what he said. He took us first to one man, who took some money off Mother, then to another, who Uncle Mir's friend called "the fixer," who took even more money off her.

I didn't like any of these people. I didn't trust them either. They treated us as if we were dirt. I felt lost in a strange and hostile world, with no Shadow to guide us anymore. But I had my silver star. I kept it hidden in my pocket. I never took it out in case someone saw it. I'd squeeze on it tight whenever I was frightened, which was a lot of the time, and always before I went to sleep at night. It was my talisman, my lucky charm.

Uncle Mir's friend kept telling us everything would be all right, that we would be looked after now all the way to England. Travel, food, we'd have everything we needed. There would be no problems, he said, no problems at all.

We believed him. We trusted him. We had to. We didn't have a choice, did we? But it turned out to be the beginning of a nightmare. They took us down into a cellar and said we'd have to stay there till everything was arranged. We were there for days on end. They gave us food and water, but they wouldn't let us out, except to go to the toilet. Mother said it was like being back in the police cell in Afghanistan.

Then they came for us one night, took us out into a dark alleyway and shoved us into the back of a pickup truck. I remember looking out of the back and seeing all the bright lights of the city. Once, when we were waiting at traffic lights, I said to Mother that we should climb out and make a run for it, that we were better off on our own. But then the truck moved off and the chance to escape was gone.

We never had another one.

Somewhere on the edge of the city, the pickup stopped. There were people waiting for us. They made us get out and climb up into the inside of a huge truck. It looked empty at first, but it wasn't. At the back, there was a large metal container, its doors wide-open. They pushed us in, threw us a couple of blankets, told us we had to be quiet and just left us. It was pitch-black in there, and cold. We sat huddled in the corner, Mother telling me all the time it was going to be all right, that Uncle Mir knew what he was doing, that these were good people who were looking after us and that everything would turn out fine, God willing.

Hours later, when we heard the sound of voices outside, and when the truck started up and moved off, I began to believe she was right, right about everything, that maybe the worst was over. I kept telling myself that we would soon be in England with Uncle Mir and we would have a warm place to sleep, running water, television, and I could go to see Manchester United play and see Ryan Giggs. I might even meet him.

But it wasn't only those thoughts that kept me going, it was my silver star and the memory I had in my head of Shadow, always trotting on ahead of us, her tail waving us on, how she'd stop to look back at us from time to time to make sure we were coming, her eyes telling us that all we had to do was to keep going like she was. I just had to think about her, picture her in my mind and, however hungry or cold or frightened I was, it made me feel a little better for a while, but not for long.

I was half asleep by the time the truck stopped

again. We heard footsteps inside the truck, then voices right outside our container. "Police," Mother whispered. "It's the police. They've found us. Please God, no. Please God, no." She had her arms around me, holding me tight, kissing me and kissing me, as if it was for the last time.

THE LITTLE RED TRAIN

Aman

The door of the container opened. The daylight blinded us. We could not see who it was at first.

It was not the police.

It turned out to be the fixer man and his gang, the same people who had put us in there. They said we could get out if we wanted and stretch our legs, that we were waiting for some other people to join us.

We were in a kind of loading bay with trucks all around, but not many people. We should have run off there and then, but one of the fixer's gang always seemed to be watching us, so we didn't dare.

Only a few minutes later and it was too late.

The other refugees arrived and we were all

herded back into the same container, given some more blankets, a little fruit and a bottle or two of water. They slammed the doors shut on us again and the fixer shouted at us that, no matter what, we mustn't call out or we'd all be caught and taken to prison. We could hear the truck being loaded up around us.

It was a while, I remember, before my eyes became accustomed to the dark again and I could see the others again.

As the truck drove off, we sat there in silence for a while, just looking at one another. I counted twelve of us in all, mostly from Iran, and a family—mother, father and a little boy—from Pakistan and beside us an old couple from Afghanistan, from Kabul.

It was Ahmed, the little boy from Pakistan, who got us talking. He came over to me to show me his toy train, because I was the only other kid there, because I knew I could trust him, I think—it was plastic and bright red, I remember, and he was very proud of it.

He knelt down to show me how it worked on the floor, and telling everyone about how his grandpa worked on the trains in Pakistan. And in secret, I showed him the silver star badge Sergeant Brodie had given me. Ahmed loved looking at it. He was full of questions about it, about everything. He liked me, he said, because I had a name that sounded like his. It wasn't long before we were all telling one another our stories. To begin with, Ahmed and me, we laughed a lot, and played around, and that cheered everyone up. But it didn't last. I think our laughter lasted about as long as the fruit and water.

I don't know where that truck took us, nor how many days and nights we were locked up in the container. They didn't let us out, not once, not to go to the toilet even, nothing. And we didn't dare shout out. They brought us no more water, no more food. We were freezing by night and stifling hot by day.

When I was awake, I just longed to be asleep, so I could forget what was happening, forget how much I was longing every moment for water and for food. Waking up was the worst. When we talked among one another now, it was usually to guess where we were, whether we were still in Iran, or in Turkey, or maybe in Italy. But none of this made any sense to me, because I had no idea where any of these places were.

Most of them, like Ahmed and his parents, said they were trying to get to England, like we were, but a few were going to Germany or Sweden. One or two had tried before, like the old couple from Kabul who were going to live with their son in England, they told us, but they had already been caught twice and sent back. They were never going to give up trying, they said.

But in the end the stories stopped altogether and there was no more talking, just the sound of moaning and crying, and praying. We all prayed. For me the journey in that truck was like traveling through a long, dark tunnel with no light at the end of it. And there was no air to breathe either, that was the worst of it. People were coughing and choking and Ahmed was being sick too. But he still held on to his little red train.

The smell, I'll never forget the smell.

After that I think I must have lost consciousness, because I don't remember much more. When I woke up—it was probably days later, but I don't know—the truck had stopped. Maybe it was the shouting and the crying that woke me up, because that was all I could hear. Mother and the others were on their feet and banging on the side of the container, screaming to be let out.

By the time they came for us and dragged me out of there, I was half dead.

But I was luckier than little Ahmed.

When his father carried him out into the daylight, we could see for sure that he was dead. Ahmed's mother was wailing in her grief. It was like a cry of pain from deep inside her, a crying that I knew would never end for her. I never heard such a dreadful sound before and I hope I never will again.

Later that same day, after they had buried him, his mother gave me his toy train to look after, because I had been like a brother to Ahmed, she said.

I've still got Ahmed's little red train, back home in Manchester. The police, when they came to take us away, wouldn't let me bring it with me. I forgot it and wanted to go back for it, and they wouldn't let me. There wasn't time, they said. It's on the windowsill in my bedroom.

I dream about Ahmed quite a bit and often it's

almost the same dream. He's with Shadow, and with Sergeant Brodie, and they're playing together outside the walls of a castle. It's night and the sky is a ceiling painted with stars, and he's throwing a ball for her.

Strange that, how in dreams people who never even knew each other can meet up in places they could never have been to.

ALL BROTHERS AND SISTERS TOGETHER

Aman

Mother told me when we got out of that truck, that we were in Turkey.

I didn't much care where we were, to be honest. Everything is a bit of a blur after that. I was ill, I remember that, but there was a lot I don't want to remember. There were more journeys by truck, one by sea when we were all seasick, but even then it was never as terrible as that one in the container. Like a black hole, it was in there.

We went in more pickups after that. We even went on horseback once, over the mountains, it was—I don't know what mountains. We slept in a shepherd's hut once, and we were stuck in there for days, because it was snowing hard outside. But I was used to snow. We had plenty of that back in Bamiyan. And the stars shine brighter when there's snow on the ground and the sky seems closer.

We traveled on foot too, dodging border patrols by night. I heard shooting once, but our guide said they did that just to frighten people away from the border. We kept going and somehow we got through. Mother always knew how. It was God watching over us, she said.

Then it was another long truck journey—at least they gave us food and water this time and we could breathe. It wasn't so bad by now. Maybe we were getting used to it, I don't know. By this time, we had all gotten to know one another and we knew we were all in this together. That helped a lot.

The old couple from Kabul never said very much, but they kept our spirits up, telling us day after day that we were getting there, that it wouldn't be long now. That was something we all wanted to believe and that was why we believed it, I suppose. This old couple, they took quite a liking to me, they said, because I reminded them of their son when he was little. In fact, everyone looked out for me and always saw to it that I had enough to eat and drink. I've thought a lot about why they were all so good to me. I think they did not want to see another child die.

In a way, I became everyone's son on that journey.

I knew, because everyone was worried about it, and talked about it all the time, that the most dangerous part of the journey was going to be the last bit, getting across the English Channel. The only way across was to hide away in a truck, I was told, and just hope not to be caught. But lots of people were caught.

Mother was terrified of being caught. It worried her all the time. It was around this time that she had her first panic attack. In a way, it was her panic attack that saved us. The old couple from Kabul looked after her and calmed her down. I think that was why they chose us, because of Mother's panic attack, and because I reminded them of their son maybe.

They had been talking about it for some time,

they told us, and they had decided they wanted to help us. They couldn't help everyone. They'd like to, but they couldn't. There were police everywhere near the French coast. They said there were hundreds of people waiting to find a way across the channel into Britain. There were plenty of fixers who would offer us a place in the back of a truck, but they were all crooks. They just wanted your money.

Well, after what happened to us before, we believed that, didn't we? The fixers might get you onto a truck, they said, but the police and immigration people were very thorough these days and they checked all the trucks, every one of them. We'd be lucky to get through. The last two times this old couple had tried, this was how they had been caught. They had a plan, they told us. It might work, it might not, but all they were sure of was that it was a lot better than chancing it again in the back of a truck. There was nothing to pay, they said, when Mother asked them. We were all Afghans, weren't we? All brothers and sisters together.

So I'll tell you how we came into England, shall I? We hung around for a long time with lots of refugees like us. It was in a kind of camp—near the sea in France. It wasn't too bad. We had food. We had shelter. We all lived in lots of tents inside a great big building.

Mother and me and the old couple from Kabul shared a tent together. Best of all, there were dozens of other kids, so we could play football. Sometimes we would pick up teams—you know, Manchester United against Barcelona. You can guess which side I played for.

The old couple had a mobile phone, so Mother spoke a couple of times on their phone to Uncle Mir in Manchester and I did too, just once. He told me that Manchester United had won the day before. They'd beaten Liverpool 2–0, and Ryan Giggs had been the best player on the pitch, and he said how much he was looking forward to taking me to see Manchester United play and having us living with him and Mina in their home.

I remember Mother was terrified the night we escaped from the camp. I was just excited. All four of us went together, the old couple from Kabul and us, and we weren't the only ones getting out that night. We crawled through a hole in the fence and ran off into the dark of the countryside. We seemed to be walking forever after that. There were dogs barking, I remember that, and it sounds stupid, but I really did wonder, just for a moment, if Shadow had followed us all this way and tracked us down with her sniffer nose. Stupid or what?

Then we came down a track and out onto a little road. We followed this for a while, until we came to a crossroads. Only minutes later this car came along, pulling a trailer. The driver turned out to be the son of the old couple, the one who was like me when he was little, they reminded me. It was all so quick. He helped all four of us up into the trailer and made us crawl in under the bed, where we all squeezed in together. Then the door was shut on us and we heard it lock. "If we are lucky," said the old man, "we will be in England in a couple of hours, maybe less. No one must talk, not a word."

Well, we didn't talk and no one discovered us. So that's how we came into England, smuggled in the back of a trailer. Uncle Mir and Aunt Mina met up with us at some gas station—I suppose everything had all been arranged with Mother on the phone. We said good-bye to the old couple and Uncle Mir drove us home to Manchester in his taxi. He was just as chatty as he had been on the phone. He was so pleased to see us that he talked almost the whole way.

The next day Uncle Mir took us into the police station in Manchester, to claim asylum, to register as asylum seekers. The sooner you do that the better, he said. Mother and me, we were so happy. We thought that was it. We'd made it to England. We thought we were safe now.

But we weren't safe at all.

"IT'S WHERE WE BELONG NOW"

Aman

All that was nearly six years ago now. And the six years have been good too. Uncle Mir has looked after us all this time, just like he said he would. I don't know what we'd do without him.

But he's been in hospital for an operation, so that's why he can't come to see us in here. He will come when he's better, he says—if we're still here, that is. He phones us every day. We've been living in a little flat, right above Uncle Mir and Aunt Mina, and his taxicab office is right next door. He gets me to man the phone in there sometimes with Aunt Mina, just to help out. It's good fun. I like it.

I like this country too. Well, I did till four weeks and six days ago when they brought us in here.

Back home in Manchester, we've got just about everything we need, enough to eat, running water and hot water too. It's a little different from the cave in Bamiyan. Once a week Uncle Mir takes me to the mosque and about once a month we go to watch Manchester United. You can't go more often than that—it's too expensive.

Uncle Mir treats me like a son. We play Monopoly, Scrabble, chess—you name it, we play it. He loves board games. I beat him at Monopoly, like I beat you. But he always beats me at Scrabble. One day I'll beat him though. And I did see Ryan Giggs. I didn't shake his hand, but I nearly did. I got his autograph instead.

But I had my ups and downs, especially to begin with. Some of the kids at primary school gave me a hard time at first. I didn't speak English, not at all to start with. So that was a bit difficult, but I soon picked it up. Then there was this mouthy kid— Dan Smart, he was called—and he picked on me in the playground. He kept pushing me around and telling me to go back to my own country. But Matt soon sorted him out, faced him down and told him he was a loser and an idiot—and lots of other names too that I had better not say. Dan didn't bother me again. And Matt and me, we've been best friends ever since. So school's great, no problems, not anymore.

But it hasn't been that easy for Mother. She misses Bamiyan a lot more than I do. She misses her friends most, I think. She still cries a lot when she thinks about Grandmother and Father and everything that happened. She helps out a friend in the charity shop down the road and she does all their mending for them on her sewing machine. She's brilliant on her sewing machine. And she teaches Dari, gives lessons to some of the local kids—but not for money. You're not allowed to earn money, not if you're an asylum seeker. But she still gets frightened sometimes and the doctor makes her take some pills. But then she gets sleepy, so she doesn't like taking them. She makes me work hard at school because she wants me to have a good job when I grow up and not be poor.

I go to school at Belmont Academy now. I like just about everything, except home economics. I've got my GCSEs next year and I'm doing my math this year, a year early, because I'm good at math.

Mr. Bell—he's my math teacher—says I'll be good enough to go to university later, if I work hard. I'm going to take my math GCSE exam in the summer, a year early. That was the plan anyway. Mother wants me to go to university as well, so that I can become an engineer, which is what I want to be. I want to build bridges. I love bridges. I'm not much good at English. I can speak it okay, but my spelling's no good.

But I've got to tell you that I'm a whole lot better at my football. I showed you the photo, didn't I, that one my football team sent me, remember? We won the league last year and the year before. We're the best! And I'm not just saying that. We are the best!

But ever since we've been living here in England, there's been one thing worrying us all the time: whether or not we'd be allowed to stay, whether the government would grant us asylum. It's been like a shadow hanging over us. I think I got used to it, but Mother could never stop thinking about it. Uncle Mir kept telling her that everything would be all right, that the lawyer said we had done everything we should have done, that we had a very good chance, that we should just get on with our lives and not worry.

But that's easier said than done. For six years we never heard anything from the government.

Then one day we get this letter, telling us we have to go back to Afghanistan, just like that. So we try to appeal. We tell them how it was for us and our family in Afghanistan, how the police treated us, how the Taliban are everywhere, how Father was killed for helping the Americans, how they murdered Grandmother. We tell them again how Mother was tortured by the police.

We have told them all this before, but it is no good. They give us all sorts of reasons. Afghanistan is different now, they tell us. It's all quite safe now, they say, and the police there aren't like they were. But we've got friends there and they all say that the Taliban are still strong and the police are just as bad as they ever were. There's a war going on over there, or don't they realize?

But they don't listen. They just want to find any reason they can to get rid of us—that's what it feels like to us anyway. We say we are proper asylum seekers, that this is our home now. This is where we belong. But they don't want to know and, like I told you, they won't even let us appeal.

Mother was always getting herself really stressed out with all this. Sometimes she couldn't sleep, she couldn't eat, and then sooner or later she'd get one of her panic attacks. I tried not to think about any of it, just put everything out of my mind, to do my work, play my football and get on with my life, like Uncle Mir told us.

But Mother could never do that. That's why I didn't pay her much attention, when she kept going on about it. She did warn me only a few months back that sooner or later they would come for us. I just always thought it would be later, or that they might forget all about us, that it might never even happen. I just didn't want to believe it, that's the truth of it.

Then one morning—I was still in bed and asleep—I was woken up by a loud knocking on the door downstairs that went on and on. It was like the beginning of your worst nightmare.

LOCKED UP

Aman

I thought it was Uncle Mir at first. Only a few days before we'd had a pipe that burst in our flat and the water had flooded down through the floor into their place. I thought it must have happened again. So I got out of bed to open the door.

But it wasn't our door and it wasn't Uncle Mir. The knocking was coming from downstairs, from the street door.

So I went down to open it. It was men in uniform, policemen, some of them were, or immigration officers maybe—I didn't know—but lots of them, ten, maybe twelve.

They pushed past me and charged up the stairs. Then one of them had me by the arm and was dragging me upstairs. I found Mother sitting up in her bed. I could see she was finding it hard to breathe and that any minute she'd be having one of her panic attacks. A policewoman was telling her to get dressed, but she couldn't move.

When I asked what was going on, they just told me to shut up. Then they were shouting at Mother, telling her we had five minutes to get ready, that we were illegal asylum seekers, that they were going to take us to a detention center, and then we'd be going back to Afghanistan. That was when I suddenly became more angry than frightened. I shouted back at them. I told them that we'd been living here six years, that it was our home. I told them to get out.

Then they got really mad. One of them pushed me out of Mother's room, and back into my bedroom, and told me to get dressed.

They never left us alone after that.

They wouldn't even go while we were getting dressed—Mother said afterward that there were at least three of them in her room all the time, one of them a man. They hardly let us take anything with us—one small rucksack and my schoolbag, that's all. Almost all of our stuff got left behind, my cell phone, all my football programs, my reading books, my Ryan Giggs autograph, Ahmed's little red engine and my goldfish.

But I had my silver star badge in my jeans pocket, so at least I didn't leave that behind. They never stopped hassling us. They took us down the stairs and out into the street. There were lots of people out there in their dressing gowns, watching us—Uncle Mir and Matt and Flat Stanley too. Matt called out to me, and asked what was going on, and I told him that they were sending us back to Afghanistan.

A policeman had me by the arm the whole time, pushing me, frog-marching me. It made me feel ashamed and I had nothing to be ashamed about. Mother was having a proper fit by now, but they didn't bother. The policewoman said she was just pretending, putting it on.

They shoved us in this van, locked us up in separate compartments, with bars on the windows, and then drove us off. I could hear Mother crying the whole time. They must have been able to hear her too, but it was just a job to them. They were busy listening to their radio and laughing.

I kept talking to Mother, trying to calm her down, but I could tell she was just getting worse and worse. I banged on the door, and screamed at the police in the front, and in the end they did stop. They had a look at Mother, and the same police-woman told me again that she was playacting, and to shut my mouth or I'd be in trouble. I didn't keep my mouth shut. I told them I wanted to be in with Mother and kept on and on until they let me. Mother calmed down a bit after that, but she was still in a really bad state when we got here.

They wanted Mother and me to be in different rooms. They said I was too old to be in with her. I told them I was staying with her, to look after her, no matter what, that I'd been with her all my life and there was no way we were going to be parted. We said we'd both go on hunger strike if they did that. We made such a fuss and noise about it that in the end they let us stay together. That was when we learned not to give in, not ever.

When I first came into this place, I couldn't be-lieve it. I mean, it looks like it might be all right from the outside, like a recreation center, a bit like my school. But inside it's all locked doors and guards.

It's all a fake, just to make it look good—fake flowers on the table, pretty pictures on the walls, a nursery, and places the kids can play and television. But it's a prison. That's what it is, a prison. That's what I couldn't believe. They put us in a prison. We were locked up. I hadn't done anything wrong, and nor had Mother, nor had anyone else in here. Everyone's got a right to ask for asylum, to try to find a safe place to live, haven't they? That's all we've done.

For the first few days in here, Mother just cried and cried. Uncle Mir came to visit and he said he'd get the lawyer and he'd do all he could to get us out of here and back home. But nothing could stop Mother from crying. When we heard the news that Uncle Mir had had a heart attack and was in hospital—on account of everything that had gone on, I suppose—it only made it worse for her. The doctor came and gave her an injection, and after that, instead of crying, she just lay there looking at the ceiling, as if she'd no feelings left inside her.

It's worse for her than it is for me. She's got her memories, of the prison they took her to back in Afghanistan. I know they're terrible memories because she still won't talk about them. She says

131

she's never, ever going back to Afghanistan, that she'd rather kill herself. And I know she means it too.

That's almost it, the whole story—oh yes, except for one thing. About a week ago, I think it was. They came into our room one morning early and told us they were going to take us to the airport, then fly us back to Afghanistan. We asked them when it was going to happen, and they told us it was right now, and we had to get ready.

We refused.

Mother fought them and so did I. They had to hold us down and handcuff us. And in the van all the way to the airport we hammered on the side of the van and we shouted and we screamed. They drove us right to the plane and tried to make us walk up the steps. We wouldn't go. They had to half drag, half carry us up. Even in her seat on the plane Mother wouldn't stop fighting them. I had almost given up by then, but Mother never did. That's why we're still here, because Mother didn't give up.

In the end, the pilot came along and said he couldn't take off with Mother and me on board, that we were a danger to the other passengers, that we were frightening them. So they took us off the plane and brought us back here. They weren't at all pleased to see us. Our wrists hurt, where they'd handcuffed us, and we were a bit bruised all over, but we didn't mind. Mother told me that night that Grandfather would have been proud of us. He had been a fighter for freedom, and so had Father, in his own way. We must fight for our freedom and never give in.

"WE'RE GOING
TO DO IT!"

Grandpa

A man turned to her. "That is what you said, Mother, isn't it? We must never give in, right?"

He still spoke in English, but I could see from her smile that she understood, that she had understood everything all along.

Aman went on, holding her hand tight in his. "They will come and try to take us away again. It could be today. It could be tomorrow, it could be next week. But we won't go without a fight, will we, Mother?" She reached out and touched the back of his head, stroking his hair fondly, proudly.

"She won't answer me," Aman said. "It's a rule she made when we came here, that with her I must always speak Dari. She says I must never forget we are Hazara, and if I speak the language, I never will. And I tell her we have to speak English because we are now English also. We are both. We argue about it, don't we, Mother?"

But I had the impression that his mother wasn't listening to him anymore. She was directing her gaze at me.

And then she spoke to me, in English, slowly, hesitantly, searching for the words, but meaning every one of them. "Thank you for coming to see us. Aman has talked about you. He likes you. You have been very kind to us."

My attention was distracted then, as it had been off and on all afternoon during Aman's story, by a little girl, only about two or three years old, I guessed, in a pink dress. She'd been running around the visitors' room and I had noticed her before, how every time the door that led to the outside world opened, whenever someone came in or went out, she would run toward it, only to have it slam shut in her face.

There were several doors out of the room, but she seemed to know that this was the door you had to go through if you wanted to get out of this place. After she found it shut against her this time, she stood there looking up at it, then at the guard standing beside it. She sat down on the floor then, a teddy in her hand, her thumb in her mouth, waiting for the door to open again, the guard looking down at her stone-faced. He kept fingering the bunch of keys on his belt, shaking them every now and again, like a rattle.

I got up to go a few moments later. "I'll be back," I told them.

"I hope we'll still be here," said Aman. I wasn't expecting him to want to shake hands. But he did. As I took his hand, I felt something pressing into mine. I guessed at once it was the silver badge. He looked hard at me, telling me with his eyes not to look down, just to put my hand in my pocket and walk away. I knew as I left the detention center, as the gates closed behind me, and I was once again out in the free world, that I was holding their future in the palm of my hand.

Matt was waiting for me with Dog. "Well? What happened, Grandpa? You've been in there ages. Did you see him?"

"I saw him, him and his mother," I said.

"Is he all right?" he asked.

"For now," I said.

Matt was bursting to hear what had happened in there. I gave him Aman's silver star badge and all the way home in the car, with Dog leaning his head on my shoulder as usual, I told him everything Aman had told me, about Bamiyan, the whole incredible story of their escape from Afghanistan, about Shadow and Sergeant Brodie, their nightmare of a journey to England—everything about Yarl's Wood too, what it was like inside—and about that little girl in the pink dress. I just couldn't get her out of my mind.

Until I'd finished—and we were nearly home by then—he said nothing, asked no questions, but simply sat there and listened, Aman's silver star badge cupped in his hands.

"He never told me," Matt said. "He never told me a thing." And then, "I've seen that little red train. He keeps it in his room. I thought it was just his favorite toy, y'know, from when he was little. He never said."

We didn't talk much after that, hardly a word till we arrived home. Then we just sat there in the car for a while. I knew what he was thinking and I think he knew what I was thinking too.

"It's no good, Matt," I told him. "I've racked my brains, but it's hopeless. Even if we could think of something, it would be too late. I really don't think there's anything we can do for them."

"Oh, yes, there is, Grandpa," Matt said. "There has to be. And we're going to do it too."

SHOOTING STARS

Matt

've got to be honest.

As I was listening to Grandpa in the car, I was feeling more and more hurt.

I mean, why hadn't Aman told me any of this before? After all, I was his best friend, wasn't I? Didn't he trust me?

Yes, of course I knew that he'd come over from Afghanistan when he was little. But I'd never asked him anything about it—I didn't think it was my business—and he'd never told me.

And yes, I knew his dad was dead, he'd told me that much, but never how he'd died, nothing about the caves, or the dog or the soldiers, nothing about being an asylum seeker. All this time, for six years, he'd told me nothing. I'd never even heard of his silver star badge before, and now here I was, holding it in my hands.

But then as the car journey went on, I felt the hurt inside me turning to anger; not anger at Aman, but anger at the way he and his mother were being treated in that Yarl's Wood place.

It was unfair. It was cruel. And it wasn't right.

The more I thought about it, the clearer my thinking became. So by the time Grandpa and I got back home, by the time we were sitting down at the kitchen table and he was pouring himself a cup of tea, I knew exactly what we should do. I didn't know if it would work. I only knew we had to try.

And what's more, I knew Grandpa would go along with it, that he was feeling just as angry about it all as I was. Even as I was telling him about my idea, I had the distinct impression that this was nothing new to him. It was something he'd already been thinking about.

"You know what I think, Grandpa?" I was telling him. "I think you should write Aman's story, put it in the newspapers, I mean. You're a journalist, aren't you? You could do it. If people knew Aman's story,

what he and his mother lived through, how he saved
Shadow and those soldiers, they'd be just as angry
about it as we are. We could get people to come to
Yarl's Wood to demonstrate, to protest. They'd come,
I know they would. I mean the government—or
whoever—they'd have to change their minds,
wouldn't they? We could do it, Grandpa."

Grandpa sipped his tea thoughtfully for a while.
"Do you really think there's a chance?" he said.

I put Aman's star on the table in front of him.
"Aman thinks so, Grandpa," I said. "That's why he
gave you this. He's relying on us, Grandpa. He's got
no one else."

Grandpa looked at me across the table. "All right.
You're on," he said. "Let's do it."

He got up right away and went into the next
room to call his old editor at the newspaper. They
talked, but not for long.

I thought from the downcast look on his face as
he came back into the kitchen that maybe he'd been
turned down. "I don't know if I can do it, Matt," he
said. "He likes the idea of the story, really excited
about it. He says if I get it right it could be front

page. But if we want it in tomorrow's paper, he says I've got two hours to get it done. Fifteen hundred words and he has to have it by six o'clock at the very latest."

"So?" I said with a shrug. "What's your problem, Grandpa? How many times have you told me to stop procrastinating and get on with my homework?"

"I take your point," Grandpa replied with a smile.

He sat down at the laptop at the kitchen table and got to work. From then on he hardly looked up. I wanted to read it over his shoulder, as he was writing, but he wouldn't let me. Only when he'd checked it through and put in the last period did he let me read it at last.

"Well?" he asked.

"Brilliant," I said. And it was too. I had tears in my eyes by the time I'd finished reading it. He e-mailed it to the newspaper at once. There was an e-mail back within minutes.

It read:

Going in the paper tomorrow. Haven't changed a word. Front page, photos, the lot.

Your headline too. "We want you back." And the byline you asked for, and with the special appeal for everyone to come along and join the protest at Yarl's Wood at 8 o'clock tomorrow. This paper is right behind you. Good luck with it.

I rang home straight after that and told Mum what Grandpa and I were up to, about everything that had happened that day, about how Grandpa's story was coming out in the newspaper the next day.

It was a long phone call and Grandpa had a word with her too. But by the end of it, when she'd heard all about Aman, she wanted to do anything she could to help and so did Dad. They agreed to contact everyone we knew: family, friends, school—by e-mail, Twitter, Facebook, text, phone, whatever way they could—to try to persuade them to come and join in the protest.

Mum was really fired up about it. She'd been quite an activist when she was a student, she said. She knew how to do these things. And they'd be there the next day themselves at Yarl's Wood, supporting us—of course they would.

Dad came on the phone then and said he was really proud of me. (I really liked him saying that. I don't think he'd ever said it before.) He sounded quite choked up and said there were times when it was good to be a troublemaker and that this was one of them—but I wasn't to make a habit of it!

So Grandpa and I left all that side of things, the organization of the protest, to Mum and Dad, and busied ourselves on the kitchen floor, making the banners. We spread newspaper out wall to wall. I found a leftover pot of green paint, out in the garden shed. It wasn't the best of colors, but it did the job. We made two. One read (my idea): WE WANT AMAN BACK. The other (Grandpa's idea): LET OUR CHILDREN GO.

It took a lot longer than we thought. It didn't help at all that Dog kept walking all over the banners, punctuating the letters with his great, green smudgy paws. We kept trying to shoo him away, but he kept coming back. He thought it was a game and there was nothing we could do to convince him it wasn't. After that we went out in the garden and sat and looked up at the stars for a while by

Grandma's tree. There were shooting stars that night, lots of them. We counted six before we went to bed. But it was the one I had in my hand that mattered most, the one I was squeezing hard and wishing on, with every shooting star we saw.

"JUST TWO OF THEM
AND A DOG"

Matt

A few hours later—and I hardly slept at all that night—we were up and on the road to Yarl's Wood Detention Center, our banners rolled up in the trunk, with Dog in the backseat panting with excitement on Grandpa's neck. He knew something was up.

We picked up a couple of copies of the morning paper from the shop on the corner and there it was, Aman's story, on the front page. We could not have hoped for more.

"Well," Grandpa said, "hopefully, hopefully that should stir things up a little. There should be quite a few ministers up in London choking on their cornflakes this morning over this!"

We both expected there to be dozens of people waiting outside the gates of Yarl's Wood when we arrived. But there was no one there. I couldn't understand it. Grandpa said it was early still, that I shouldn't worry, that they'd be along soon enough. But I was on my cell phone right away, making sure Mum and Dad at least were on their way. They weren't answering and that made me even more anxious and depressed.

Feeling a bit ridiculous now, and sad, we stood there, the two of us and Dog outside the barbed wire fence at Yarl's Wood, holding up our banners, waiting and hoping someone would notice us, that we wouldn't be alone like this for long. We were hopeful every time a car came up the road, but everyone just drove past us and in through the gates. We got a lot of strange looks.

The security people on the gates came to have a look at us through the wire, and we could see them then on the phone back in their guardroom. At least they'd noticed us, I thought, that was something. But, an hour or so later, and a long hour it was too, no one had come to join us. Grandpa, I could tell, was trying not to look too disappointed, but he was, and I was too.

"Not exactly a mass protest, is it?" I said.

"Give it time, Matt, give it time," Grandpa told me.

I knew he was only trying to make the best of it, trying to make me feel better, and that really began to irritate me in the end. He said that it wasn't even breakfast time for most people yet, that it would all turn out fine.

"No, it won't," I snapped. "Course it won't, not if no one comes." I went off to take Dog for a run, partly because I could see he was getting fed up standing there on the lead, but mostly because I was ashamed of myself for having snapped at Grandpa. I let Dog off the lead and we ran off together down the wide grass shoulder of the road.

I was back with Grandpa, still trying to find a way to say sorry, when, at long last, we saw a car coming slowly up the road. It stopped and parked up on the shoulder. Our first protester, I thought. But it was a police car. Two policemen got out and came over to us, one of them talking on his radio as he came. I heard him saying something like: "Nothing to worry about. Just two of them and a dog."

They came up and asked Grandpa what we were doing there. Grandpa gave it to them straight. I was amazed at him. I'd never seen him angry and defiant like this before. He told them about Aman, about all the kids and families being kept locked up in there, and about how it was wrong and cruel. I just went on where he left off. I was really fired up.

"How would you like it," I said, "if your kids were locked up like that when they'd done nothing wrong? My best friend's in there and any day now they're going to send him back to Afghanistan. He's been living here six years! That's why we're protesting about it."

I think they were a bit taken aback. They took our names and then said it was all right for us to stay, just so long as we didn't block the road and didn't cause a public nuisance—whatever that meant. They went away then, but only so far as their car, from where they sat and watched us. That made me feel all the more silly, because I knew they must be laughing at us.

We'd been there for over two hours. I still

couldn't get hold of Mum and Dad on the cell. Their phones had to be switched off or out of signal. It was nearly half past ten by now, plenty of time for other people to have gotten to Yarl's Wood. I kept taking Dog for runs, to keep myself occupied, to stop myself from feeling too miserable. It didn't work. I was ready to give up.

"It's no use, Grandpa," I said. "We've got to face it. No one's read the story, and even if they have, they're not coming. There's no point in staying."

That was when Grandpa sat down, patted the grass beside him for me to do the same, and then poured us out some tea from the thermos he'd brought along. We had some cookies too, chocolate digestives, lots of them. I felt a little better already.

"You got that star with you, have you?" Grandpa asked me after a while.

"Yes," I said.

"Then give it an almighty squeeze, Matt, and just hope. That's what Aman told me he did, when things were looking really bad for him. It worked for him."

I did what he said and gripped the star hard in my pocket, till my eyes watered.

That's when we saw a black vehicle coming slowly up the hill toward us. We saw as it came closer that it was a taxi. It stopped right in front of us. On the side of the front door, it read, "MMM. Mir's Motors Manchester." Six of them got out, all Aman's family—I knew all of them—and the last was Uncle Mir, helped out by Aunt Mina.

Uncle Mir was looking frail but determined, and was leaning heavily on a stick, as he walked toward me. He shook my hand, and Grandpa's, and was full of tearful and effusive thanks for all we were doing. The whole family bustled around, helping him into a wheelchair, and wrapping him in a blanket, Aunt Mina scolding him all the time for doing this against doctor's orders.

When he was settled in his wheelchair, he told us that after he had read the piece in the newspaper, nothing on earth would have stopped him from being here. "Aman is like a son to me," he told Grandpa. "I am so proud of him and his mother too. One thing is missing, though, in your newspaper story. Didn't he tell you that he wrote to him, to the soldier, to that Sergeant Brodie?"

"No," Grandpa said. "He never told me."

"Well, he did," he went on. "Twice. Once, it was to ask if he could come to see Shadow. He worships that dog, always has—all these years later and he's still talking about her. But he didn't get an answer. Then later, he wrote to ask Sergeant Brodie to support their appeal for asylum, so that they could be allowed to stay in this country. He found out the address of the regiment, sent the letter—I posted it myself—but he never had a reply to that letter either. He kept hoping for one, but it never came. Aman found that so hard. But he was never angry about it. I was though. I tell you, if I ever meet that man, I'll give him a piece of my mind. I will."

SINGING IN THE RAIN

Matt

I mean, why?" Uncle Mir went on and he was getting more and more upset. "Why wouldn't this Sergeant Brodie write back? And when you think what Aman did that day? He saved their lives, for God's sake." His wife was trying to calm him down, but Uncle Mir wasn't listening to her. "With friends like that soldier, who needs enemies?" he said bitterly.

And then, as he was talking, I looked up and saw Dad's car coming up the road toward us, Mum waving at us out of the window. At last, at last.

They weren't alone. There was a whole convoy of cars coming along behind them, and in them at least a dozen or more of our friends from home. Mum made all sorts of excuses, terrible traffic on the highway, and the cell had run out of battery.

I didn't mind. They were here.

Suddenly I was beginning to believe this might actually work. And when, an hour or so later, a bus came up the road, and I saw what was obviously our whole football team piling out in their blue gear, Grandpa and I were jumping up and down, hugging each other and whooping with joy. It was quite a moment. Dog thought so too. He was going wild!

Flat Stanley was there, Samir, Joe, Solly, all of them. They all came running over. I had the whole team around me. It felt suddenly so good. Nothing could stop us now. We were going to win. We always won, didn't we?

"Quite a production you got going here," said Flat Stanley with that great big grin on his face. "For Aman, right?"

"For Aman," I said.

There were parents and teachers with them, and there were other kids there too, from our year, a whole busload!

They held up the banner we'd all made weeks ago back at school for the team photo, the one we'd sent off to Aman. WE WANT YOU BACK, it read, in letters all the colors of the rainbow, big and bold and bright.

Then the television cameras were there too, lots of them. There were newspaper reporters and radio reporters and everyone wanted to interview us. In the end, by the middle of the afternoon, just about all our friends and family had turned up to join us, just as we had hoped they would. They came from all over, most from Manchester and Cambridge, but many from much farther away.

Auntie Morag, who is eighty-four years old, had flown down from Orkney, and brought three of her friends with her, to support the best of causes, she said, as she gave me a hug. So Grandpa and I had plenty to be happy about. In all, there must have been a couple of hundred people gathered there and more were arriving all the time.

No one told anyone to start chanting, it just seemed to happen, led mostly by Flat Stanley and Samir and the football team, then picked up by all of us.

"We want Aman back! We want Aman back!"

More security people were gathering behind the

gates all the time and they were beginning to look more and more anxious, on their phones the whole time.

Apparently we had been on national television and radio for the lunchtime news, and of course the newspaper story had been out there for several hours by now, with its invitation for anyone and everyone to join us. And they were joining us now, more and more all the time, more than we could ever have believed possible. This wasn't just a small protest demonstration anymore; it was becoming a huge crowd, a shouting, chanting, arm-waving crowd. This was the real thing, a proper protest. There were enough of us there by now for everyone to know that we meant it, that we weren't going away.

But more police were arriving too, in large white vans, and when they jumped out we saw that these ones were carrying helmets and shields. I don't think I realized until I saw them quite how serious this might become, that things really could get out of hand.

All around me, feelings were running high, and I could see from the faces of the policemen that they were sensing it too. They had dogs with them and Dog did not like that one bit. He barked at them furiously if they ever came too close and I was pleased to see that the police dogs seemed a little surprised at that. They didn't seem to know quite what to do. I was proud of Dog. He wasn't going to be intimidated any more than we were.

All the pushing and shoving, all the shouting and chanting was exciting, but it was frightening too. I was beginning to wonder whether this had been such a good idea in the first place. I mean, Aman was still stuck in there, inside Yarl's Wood, and we were outside. Yes, we were making a lot of noise, and making quite a nuisance of ourselves too. But what good was it doing, and how was it going to help Aman and his mother if someone got hurt?

I could feel myself losing heart again, losing hope. I reached into my pocket and squeezed tight on Aman's star. That, and another chocolate cookie, and the high spirits of the crowd around me bucked me up enough to keep me going, keep my courage up, keep me chanting along with the others.

But then it began to rain, and rain hard, and all the chanting and the shouting soon faded away.

We were left standing there, dripping and cold, and feeling rather sorry for ourselves. It was as if the police had ordered the rain to dampen our spirits and it was working. But then Grandpa did something completely wonderful, completely surprising. He started singing, in the rain. And that *is* what he was singing too: "Singin' in the Rain," from one of his favorite films, and mine—we'd watched the DVD often together. In no time, everyone was joining in, laughing, arms linked, and singing and dancing in the rain.

Some of the police were smiling too, I noticed, but none of them was dancing.

But a song can only go on for so long and soon we were all just standing there in the rain, silent again, waiting, not knowing quite what for. I mean, we'd made our point, done our protest, but so what? Hour after hour we stood there, wet and cold and tired. No one was saying it, but I knew everyone was thinking what I was thinking. Aman and his mother were still locked up inside Yarl's Wood, and if they were coming out at all, it would only be in a car that would be taking them to the airport to deport them back to Afghanistan. Sooner or later we'd all have to go home and we would have achieved nothing. Even Aman's silver star seemed to have lost its power.

Cars and vans came and went through the gates into the detention center. More security guards were there now on the other side of the wire and I noticed a couple of them were taking photographs of us. More police reinforcements kept arriving. They were there in their hundreds now, facing us, silent and unsmiling. It was a standoff.

But they didn't scare me anymore. I think I was too cold and wet and hungry to be frightened. I couldn't help thinking that Grandpa and I hadn't thought this part of our plan through at all. We didn't have an umbrella between us, no tea left, no more cookies. And what if everyone just ignored us and left us there, getting wetter and wetter? I could feel a growing sense of the same desperation around me in the crowd. The whole protest was just fizzling out and people were starting to drift away. The football team were looking miserable and cold, as if they'd just lost 10–0. Uncle Mir had long ago been taken away to sit in his car. It was obvious that we couldn't last for much longer.

But all our hopes and spirits were raised when the rain stopped at last and the sun came out. We suddenly saw a glorious rainbow climbing up into the sky behind the detention center. "A good luck sign, if ever I saw one," said Grandpa.

When some moments later it turned out to be a double rainbow, everyone in the crowd started laughing and cheering. I had never heard a rainbow being cheered before. Like Grandpa said, a good omen. It had to be, surely.

That was when I saw one of the policemen come striding across the road toward us, purposefully, a bullhorn in his hand. "May I have your attention, please?" he began. It was a while before the crowd quieted down enough for him to go on. "I am Inspector Smallwood, and I have just been informed that Mrs. Khan and her son, Aman, left Yarl's Wood Detention Center early this morning. They were taken to Heathrow Airport to be put on a flight to Kabul. So I have to tell you that these individuals are no longer here. They have already been removed."

TIME TO GO HOME

Matt

We all stood there in stunned silence. I looked up and saw through my tears that there was a blackbird singing from the top of the barbed wire fence, the double rainbow still there arcing through the sky. It was almost as if both were mocking us.

The police officer hadn't finished. "So now you know," he said. "Which means that there's no point in hanging around here anymore. It's all over. So now, let's all go home, before we catch our death. Let's break this up. Come on, now. Time to go home."

I don't think I would have actually cried, had I not heard the sound of sobbing from among the football team standing behind me. My eyes and my heart welled up with tears then. Grandpa clung on to my arm and held it tight. There was nothing we could say.

It was over.

I didn't see or hear the car coming up the road. It just seemed to be there, in front of us, suddenly, out of nowhere.

I watched as the car doors opened and I was wondering who it was. But I didn't really care anymore. I was that miserable. The first to get out was a young girl, about ten or eleven years old, I thought. And then a dog jumped out after her on a lead.

It was a spaniel, a brown-and-white spaniel— like Dog. Just like Dog.

The girl was trying to hang on to the dog, at the same time as reaching in to help a man out of the backseat. As he got out and stood up, I saw that he was a soldier, in a khaki uniform and a cap. He had medals, lots of them. He was walking with a stick and gazing around him, strangely. I knew at once that he was looking about him like blind men do, looking without seeing.

The girl was still struggling to hold on to her dog.

"Grandpa," I whispered. "That's Sergeant Brodie, isn't it? And that's got to be Shadow. It has to be."

Everyone seemed to realize who they were by now—from Grandpa's story in the paper, I suppose—and the whole crowd began clapping. The two dogs, Shadow and Dog, were nose to nose, tails wagging wildly.

"Sorry we're late," the soldier was saying. "Traffic, and everything up in London took a whole lot longer than I thought it would, didn't it, Jess? Oh, this is Jess, my daughter. And I'm Sergeant Brodie, by the way. I'm an old friend of Aman's." Shadow and Dog were sniffing each other over and squeaking with excitement.

For a long while we all just stood there, not knowing quite what to say. Then Grandpa spoke up. "I'm afraid it's too late," he said. "They've just told us here that Aman and his mother were taken away this morning, before we got here. They're already on their way back to Afghanistan. We're all too late."

Shadow was snuffling busily around my feet now. "Sorry about her," Jess said, fighting to pull her back. "Shadow goes where her nose goes, she's like that." Dog wouldn't leave Shadow alone. He thought he had found a friend for life, a fellow sniffer, a fellow wagger.

"Oh, but we're not too late," said Sergeant Brodie with a smile. "You obviously haven't heard the news, have you?"

"What news?" I asked.

"About the volcano," his daughter said, "up in Iceland. There's this huge cloud of ash up there in the sky and the planes can't fly, none of them can, not anywhere, not to Afghanistan, not to anywhere. All the airports are closed."

"That's right," Sergeant Brodie went on. "Better explain, I think. When Jess read me the piece in the paper this morning, I called the regiment, spoke to my commanding officer, told him the entire story—some of which he already knew, of course—and he arranged for me to go with him to London to see the minister right away."

He tapped one of the medals on his chest, a silver one. "This little gong they gave me, the Military Cross, it opens a few doors, has its uses. I always knew it was a lucky medal anyway. Plenty of the other lads deserved it as much as I did. The truth is that, without my lucky medal, and without that lucky volcano, Aman and his mother would have been long gone by now, that's for sure. Anyway, the long and the short of it is that Aman and his mother are staying. A special case, the minister called it, when he'd heard me out, a very special case. And he's dead right. Aman was a good friend to us, a good friend to the regiment, and to the army. Everyone should look after their friends, that's what I told the minister. He picked up the phone and stopped the deportation there and then. I've spoken to Aman and his mother myself, on the phone, told them the good news. I think they were quite pleased really! They're on their way back here right now."

It took a while for all this to sink in and then for the news to spread among the crowd. And when it did there was a whole lot of hugging and cheering and whooping. There was a fair bit of crying too. Everyone began singing "Singin' in the Rain" again—although it wasn't, if you see what I'm saying.

The best moment for me, for Grandpa, and for Uncle Mir and his family, for everyone in the crowd, came an hour or so later when we saw a car coming up the road toward us. We could see Aman and his mother waving to us from inside. Aman jumped out, saw Shadow, and ran over to her at once. He crouched down, put his arms around her and held her. I was right there beside them, the football team all around, all of us together again.

For several moments no one spoke. Shadow was licking Aman all over his ear, making him giggle. He looked up at his mother then. "You see, Mother, I told you she'd know me. I told you, didn't I?"

"Aman?" said the sergeant, holding out his hand toward him. Aman stood up and took his hand.

"I wrote to you," Aman said quietly. "You never wrote back."

The sergeant was frowning, touching his forehead above his eyes with the tips of his fingers, as if he was in pain. "I'm sorry, Aman," he said, "but I never got it. Stuff gets lost, I suppose, what with one thing and another. The trouble is, I've been in and out of hospitals quite a lot over the last few years. Fifteen operations in all. IED. Roadside bomb, it was. The day it happened, I didn't have Shadow with me, more's the pity. It would never have happened if she'd been there. They've been trying to patch me up ever since. Got a new leg, new arm too. They work fine. But they couldn't do anything about my eyes. I haven't been able to see a thing since the day it happened."

Aman took a step back and I could see that he was noticing the sergeant's white stick for the first time. "I'm sorry," he said. "And I've been blaming you all this time for not writing back, even hating you for it sometimes."

"You couldn't have known," the sergeant told him. "No one's fault, Aman. The bomb's fault. The war's fault. And anyway, we met up in the end, didn't we? 'Got to look on the bright side, there's always someone worse off than yourself'—that's what my gran always used to say. And she was right. It could have been a lot worse for me—for some of the lads, it was a lot worse. When they brought me back home, after I was wounded, when I was in hospital, I told Jess all about you and Shadow and she decided to call her Shadow from then on. She couldn't be Polly to either of us anymore. Shadow's my eyes now, and that's only thanks to you, son."

That was when Aman saw his mother wheeling Uncle Mir through the crowd toward us. He ran over to him at once. A moment or two later, crouching down by Uncle Mir in his wheelchair, Aman looked across at me and smiled. I took the silver star out of my pocket and handed it back to him. He didn't say anything, he didn't need to.

That evening, late, after it was all over, we were back at Grandpa's house, the two of us, and sitting out in the garden beside Grandma's tree. I was sad and I knew I shouldn't be. I was sad because I knew this had been the best day of my life and that there would never be another one like it.

We had fed Dog, who was lying at my feet, as usual, his head heavy on my toes. He looked sad too, I thought, probably because he was missing his new friend.

And the stars were out. They were looking down on us and we were looking up at them.

"Aren't they wonderful, Matt?" Grandpa said. "I think stars are just wonderful, don't you?"

"Yes, Grandpa," I replied. "But if you ask me, I think volcanoes are best. I think volcanoes are really great."

ACKNOWLEDGMENTS

So many have helped in the genesis of *Shadow*. First of all, Natasha Walter, Juliet Stevenson and all involved in the writing and performing of *Motherland*, the powerful and deeply disturbing play that first brought to my attention the plight of the asylum-seeking families locked up in Yarl's Wood. Then there were two remarkable and unforgettable films that inspired and informed the Afghan part of this story: *The Boy Who Plays on the Buddhas of Bamiyan*, directed by Phil Grabsky, and Michael Winterbottom's *In This World*. And my thanks also to Clare Morpurgo, Ann-Janine Murtagh, Nick Lake, Livia Firth and so many others for all they have done.

POSTSCRIPT

THE WAR IN AFGHANISTAN

The Taliban rose to power in Afghanistan in 1996 and ruled for five years. The strict regime was notorious for human rights abuses and for its extremist views prohibiting the education of women.

Following the September 11 attacks, Osama Bin Laden was declared the prime suspect by President George W. Bush. Bin Laden was thought to be in Afghanistan and the U.S. issued an ultimatum demanding that Afghanistan hand over Al-Qaeda leaders in the country. They refused, and the U.S. and UK began to bomb Afghan targets on October 7, 2001. The following month the UN authorized the institution of the International Security Assistance

Force in Afghanistan, to help maintain security in and around the capital, Kabul.

Since 2001 the balance of power in Afghanistan has shifted repeatedly, with Taliban forces gaining and losing control over different parts of the country at different times. When the invasion by U.S. and UK forces began in 2001, polls indicated that about 65 percent of Britons supported military action. However, by November 2008, 68 percent of Britons supported withdrawing troops from Afghanistan.

There are no official figures on the number of civilian casualties of the war, but some estimates run to the tens of thousands. As of August 1, 2010, 327 British military personnel had been killed while on operations in Afghanistan.

YARL'S WOOD

Yarl's Wood is an immigration removal center in Bedfordshire, UK. The center can accommodate 405 people and is the main removal center for women and families who are awaiting deportation from the UK. The complex includes health care and educational facilities for detainees.

Since Yarl's Wood opened in November 2001, a number of protests and hunger strikes have been staged by detainees at the center in response to alleged poor conditions, including separation of parents from their children and lack of access to legal representation.

A report by the chief prisons inspector found

that some children were being held at Yarl's Wood unnecessarily and raised concerns over their welfare. In July 2010, the British government pledged to end the detention of children at Yarl's Wood.

ARMY SNIFFER DOGS

Springer spaniels like Shadow are commonly used as sniffer dogs by the police, prison services and the armed forces. A sniffer dog has been trained to use its sense of smell to detect substances such as the explosives used in bombs and to signal their presence to its handler. There are about two hundred military working dogs, including sniffer dogs, in the British army, and they are trained at the Defence Animal Centre in Leicestershire and in Cyprus.

In 2010, Treo, an eight-year-old black Labrador, was awarded the Dickin Medal, the animal equivalent of the Victoria Cross, for saving soldiers' lives by detecting roadside bombs in Afghanistan on two separate occasions.

Thank you for reading this FEIWEL AND FRIENDS book.

The Friends who made

SHADOW

possible are:

Jean Feiwel, publisher
Liz Szabla, editor-in-chief
Rich Deas, creative director
Elizabeth Fithian, marketing director
Holly West, assistant to the publisher
Dave Barrett, managing editor
Lauren A. Burniac, associate editor
Nicole Liebowitz Moulaison, production manager
Ksenia Winnicki, publishing associate
Anna Roberto, editorial assistant

Find out more about our authors and artists
and our future publishing at
mackids.com.

OUR BOOKS ARE FRIENDS FOR LIFE